Hope in the Desperate Hour

BOOKS BY DAVID ADAMS RICHARDS

*The Coming of Winter* 1974
*Blood Ties* 1976
*Dancers at Night* (short stories) 1978
*Lives of Short Duration* 1981
*Road to the Stilt House* 1985
*Nights Below Station Street* 1988
*Evening Snow Will Bring Such Peace* 1990
*For Those Who Hunt the Wounded Down* 1993
*Hope in the Desperate Hour* 1996

# Hope in the Desperate Hour

A  NOVEL  BY

David Adams Richards

M&S

**Canadian Cataloguing in Publication Data**

Richards, David Adams, 1950–
    Hope in the desperate hour

ISBN 0-7710-7459-X

I. Title.

PS8585.I17H6 1996     C813'.54     C95-933342-8
PR9199.3.R33H6 1996

The author wishes to thank his editor, Ellen Seligman

The publishers acknowledge the support of the Canada Council and
the Ontario Arts Council for their publishing program.

Typesetting by M&S, Toronto
Printed and bound in Canada on acid-free paper

McClelland & Stewart Inc.
*The Canadian Publishers*
481 University Avenue
Toronto, Ontario
M5G 2E9

1  2  3  4  5     00  99  98  97  96

*For Liz and Ray Mitchell*

"Every sin is the result of a collaboration."
                                        – Stephen Crane

Hope in the Desperate Hour

At five o'clock on Holy Thursday morning it was snowing, snow dawdling down over the reserve. Peter Bathurst woke as men do when they are worried. The same thoughts from the previous night's worry come back.

Peter owed money. And his enemies – those who had once been his friends – had found it out. Since Peter had failed to get re-elected to the band council a month ago, the new chief had checked into the accounts and trust funds and the council had demanded thirty thousand dollars by Good Friday. It was now Holy Thursday.

At any time in the last five years Peter could have gone to the band office and opened up the secret large box with his keys and have taken money. He would have been able to use his card, and draw money from an account. Now these solutions were far, far out of his grasp. For the last few days, he was beginning to feel the awful effects of his new position.

Peter turned over on the bed and stared at his wrist – thickened by years of hard work and fights.

He thought back again to three years ago. He had met Mickey Dunn one afternoon and had had a casual conversation with him which, at the time, didn't seem that important.

"Do you want to make a million dollars?" Mickey had asked suddenly.

"Everyone wants to make a million dollars," Peter had answered, laughing and trying to look very dignified.

Mickey then took him to Drummondville, in the province of Quebec.

They went to a crowded motel, met a French man who talked about a casino on the reserve and how they would all make millions.

There was another man there, a man from Devon whom Mickey Dunn knew and said he trusted. This man wore his hair slicked back and he tried to be very comical. But Peter knew that he and the man from Devon instantly disliked each other.

It was not the first time a casino had been spoken about. In the previous two band elections, a casino had been sought. On previous occasions Peter had been against it. However, Mickey Dunn – Mickey Dunn – convinced him this time that the profits would be enormous.

So, at the meeting in Drummondville, the idea of a casino, which Peter had once opposed as sinful, became morally appropriate to help his people.

Since that day the debate about the casino had raged

between two groups of natives. One group he headed; the other group was headed by a former protégé of his, Diane Bartibog.

In the past three years, Peter had taken over forty thousand dollars from the band council, and had used it to help himself, Mickey Dunn, the Devon man, and the man from Quebec. Continually he poured money into the casino project, letting Mickey advise him. The idea that it was sinful disappeared, and the more he was thwarted, the more determined he had become to succeed.

But it had not happened. He had tried to get everything in order before the election last month, but the election had come and gone. He had lost his membership on the band council. Now no one wanted the casino. They had begun to check their accounts, and check for money he had funnelled from the band.

Diane Bartibog was now the most powerful voice on the reserve, and no one was listening to him any more. Now, instead of being called a *warrior* or a *protector* he was being called a thief. Worse, someone had fired shots at Diane Bartibog's house during the heated election, wounding a child inside, and he had been blamed.

He knew it wasn't him. Peter secretly thought it may have been Diane's own husband, LeRoy Penniac, seeking publicity and support from the white press.

Five days ago, in the middle of a horrible storm, Sergeant John Delano of the local RCMP visited his house, telling him that an outside investigation into the missing funds was about to begin.

Thinking this, he rose in the dark. He had lied to Sergeant Delano five days ago. He had said the band council was hysterical, and that all the money would be forthcoming and accounted for. But he knew this was impossible.

Along the great hallway the morning air was still, and frost shone on the windowpane. He looked across the highway toward Mickey Dunn's bar, which he now silently cursed. He looked toward the end of the reserve and across the old iron bridge. There, in the dark, loomed Shackle's barn.

Peter then went into his father's room. His father was sitting on his squeaky rocking chair with the cowhide back, rocking, and looking at him, with a cigarette in his fingers.

"I want you to take the bus," he said to his father, handing him a letter. "See if you can find some help – go to St. Mary's reserve – I would help them – they know that. They all owe me money. If it wasn't for me they wouldn't even have that treaty."

He shrugged at the boast, and his father shrugged.

The old man looked at him. It was foolish to go. It was Holy Thursday.

Peter turned and walked back to his room. He closed the door tightly, went across the room and opened his bottom dresser drawer. He read over a contract on Dunn and Bathurst Enterprises paper.

The contract had been signed by Ms Vicki Shackle, for her percentage in a casino that didn't even exist yet. She had pledged twenty thousand dollars.

When everything was going well, Mickey Dunn had no intention of honouring such a contract (there was only one copy) and he had given it to Peter to hide. But now, this statement of Vicki Shackle was the only thing Peter had left. And he was determined to make her honour it.

Mickey Dunn, on Peter's behalf, had brought Vicki Shackle into his office three weeks ago. She was a slender woman, with black hair and beautiful dark eyes.

She had told them she could get the money, by Holy Thursday. She had begged them not to bother her husband or tell the police. Though she tried not to, she shook, and Peter had felt sorry for her.

The contract was bogus. It would not stand up in a court of law. Peter Bathurst knew this. And Vicki did not.

Remembering now how Vicki had shaken, sitting in Dunn's small office, when they told her she would go to jail, Peter started to tear the contract in two.

And yet he couldn't. He couldn't bring himself to.

Peter had thought of one other way to get out of this mess. But it was a way he did not consider seriously at this moment. He could reveal who had fired the shot at Diane Bartibog's house. There was a separate investigation under way, dealing with this. The little girl had had to go to the hospital with a flesh wound, and the papers still made a great deal of it.

Last night, when he was unable to sleep, he had tried to think of who could have done it. That is, he had tried to think of someone he could *blame* it on. Someone that would satisfy Diane, so she might help him. If he was to save himself in this way, he could never tell her it was her own people. Yet he suspected it was her own people.

And so, for now, this morning, this did not seem to be a possible solution.

Peter put the contract carefully into the folder and set it back in the drawer. He planned to take it to Dunn's later in the day when they would meet with Vicki. She would hand a cheque to them, they would burn the contract. In this way, her husband wouldn't have to be bothered again.

Across the small river on a small frozen patch of earth sat the Shackle barn. It had been built in 1953. It was a huge barn, dark, twisted, with small stalls, and an indoor area made into an arena. Upstairs, past pictures of three generations of draft horses that were all dead, there was a small tack room. In the great yard sat old cars, axles from cannibalized automobiles, cans of diesel gas, and an old tractor with a broken seat.

Garth and Vicki Shackle's only child, Penny, whom everyone called Pumpkin, was awake at quarter to six. She went immediately to the barn to feed the horses and turn them out.

She turned the mare out first. The stud moved impatiently, his mane falling in front of his black eyes, his coat grown out. It was difficult to get close to him for he had kicked before when the mare was near, and Pumpkin, though brave and resourceful at twenty, was tiny.

The snow fell against the back of her white neck as she let the colt run beside the mare. Everywhere the sky was lucid grey, and snow fell. The old barn loomed above her, and there was a smell of horse and steel in the wet and boggy ground.

She went back inside the barn and taking a shovel began to muck out the Arabian's stall. Her fourteen-year-old dog, Folly, hobbled after her on three legs.

The barn was quiet, poorly lighted and foggy. Steam rose feebly from a patch of manure near the wheelbarrow. The wheelbarrow was filled with damp hay crusted over with blackened sawdust.

Far across the yard she could see the small light go on in the old farmhouse, cut off from everything, and existing on a stretch of land on the opposite side of the river from a rundown Indian reserve and the small village of Taylorville.

The small light meant that her mother – Vicki Shackle – was awake.

Pumpkin turned away from that light, and continued to work.

She knew only some of the story. It was a story of suffering, of uncaring, and of misery, which no one remembered any more. Only her mother remembered it, in all its great passionate darkness, and its memory had brought her mother agony. Only her father remembered it, and it had brought him pain and suffering.

Years ago, before she was born, her father, Garth Shackle, was to be drafted by the Boston Bruins. But before his rookie season, in the late 1960s, he went to play in the world championship.

Her mother, Vicki, was desperate to marry Garth before he left. She was nineteen and kept worrying about him meeting someone else. She was a year older than he was, a beauty queen at Homecoming Days in Taylorville.

Garth had decided to tell Vicki that he would not marry her until after his first year in the pros. By that time, he felt, he would be financially secure. He went to visit her just after Christmas. She was sitting near the window in her living room, staring down at the patches of wild grass that lay uncovered in the snow. The wind blew, the windows rattled, the sides of the house were stacked up with boughs.

The small tree was still up in the corner, near the piano. The presents under that tree seemed not heartfelt, but bought within a certain budget not only economically but emotionally. Garth perhaps noticed this. Perhaps not.

He began to tell Vicki what he had decided, but when he went to sit down, she fumbled for his hand, her eyes filling with tears.

"You don't love me," she whispered.

Suddenly everything changed, and he began to say the exact opposite of what he had rehearsed.

This is what Pumpkin now knew. No one had to explain this to her anymore. Living with her parents for the last twenty years she was given the key to piecing it together – and in piecing it together, still loved them.

The wedding took place at St. Brenden's. Vicki wore a white dress with blue sequins. There was a conscious idea that she had at last proven herself to everyone in town.

This idea, however subtle, was a constant feeling through-
out the afternoon, promoted by her overweight mother in
her heavy blue dress.

It snowed and snowed that wedding afternoon, the
great yellow snowplough chugging away at the end of the
church lane.

There was champagne, sparkling on immaculate white
tables. And wine for everyone, and everyone got giddy.
The priest, a young fellow with thin hands, led them in a
song, about a true and Christian marriage.

There were huge shadows. The black trees just outside
the community centre shook in the clear startled wind.
Pumpkin remembered that she had seen that wedding
picture, faded, in a drawer upstairs, of the priest, of her
mother, turning away from the camera to smile at
someone – someone never known.

The Indian woman, Mary Francis, had helped cater,
with little Diane Bartibog, at six years of age, walking
behind her, both wearing hand-me-down dresses. Diane
in thick pink glasses, with one side taped.

Peter Bathurst kept the snow away from the doors.
Emile Dexter was best man. Mickey Dunn sent champagne.

Pumpkin knew this also: that all of these people, along
with her uncle, Professor Neil Shackle, and his friend,
Professor Wheem, would become for the rest of their lives
intrinsically linked to each other.

Only they that day didn't seem – didn't seem to know.

The bride and groom went to a hotel in Campbellton that was torn down after a fire in the 1970s.

The snow fell though the sky was clear and cold. A bottle of Canadian champagne sat in a plastic champagne bucket filled with water and ice.

Congratulations from friends and family and hangers-on like Mickey Dunn littered the bed. The curtains were white. The room had a doe-tail whiteness to it, in the thousands of tiny white orbs of paint. The TV screen was snowy, the curtains heavy, the bars of soap in small square blocks and wrapped with paper. They entered a gloomy, shadowed room, in the middle of the day.

They sat up until late at night. Garth grinning. His best man was supposed to be the great centreman, Verriker, from Sault Ste. Marie. But Verriker could not make it down on short notice to the bleak Maritimes. The stand-in was Garth's childhood friend Emile Dexter, whose father owned the one department store in the town. Vicki wanted nothing to do with Dexter and considered his being best man a bad omen. Garth asked her why.

"Well," Vicki sniffed, "he's not like us – he's not like you and I. He'll never do anything no matter how many department stores his fat dad owns."

"No no, for sure, for sure," Garth said and decided he should now take himself and life more seriously. But he was saddened a little by Vicki's conceit.

"He's more – like Neil," Vicki said, her Maritime accent heavy. She did not like Garth's brother Neil either, who had once told her that if she wanted to read, not to waste time reading nurse novels.

She frowned at this memory, and wiped some champagne from her lips, triumphantly.

She wore a navy-blue travelling suit and a small hat. Outside it began to blow. There was no bar in the hotel. Everything was locked up. They had also smuggled in a pint that Peter Bathurst had given them. Far away a light or two twinkled in the province of Quebec.

Later they went downstairs.

But the restaurant was closed, the nine tables looking desperate with their thick silverware.

They were the only two in the hotel. The Christmas tree looked sad, standing in the lobby, and New Year's decorations could be seen when they passed the open door of the small ballroom. The broken red high-heel of a woman's shoe had been left under a table.

That too seemed a bad omen to Pumpkin now.

A week after the wedding, Garth was gone to training camp. Vicki came home to live with her in-laws. She did not want to bother with her friends at that time. They all seemed to be so limited in what they would ever do.

She loved to read true romances – for she found herself in them all. She wrote poetry.

Then the word came through the static on the radio, over the dark grey Atlantic, across the snow-ridden pastures and fields, and endless nothing. The words, "*In the corner, here's Shackle, Shackle – now Rasperov – oh –*"

Garth was injured in this pre-tournament game against

the Soviets. He was checked in the neck from behind, and fell into the boards with his head down. For years people like Peter Bathurst, like Dexter, like Pumpkin's grand-father, Tom, tried to decide exactly how it had happened. Garth had gone over the boards only ten seconds before, to replace his friend Verriker. It seemed as if there was no need for this. But he had had an impulse to score. He caught a pass in his skates. He was checked by Igor Rasperov, a young boy whom Shackle had not known or heard of before that day.

Before that crosscheck, Shackle and his friend Verriker had brought their country to its feet time and again – both men unheralded and both brilliant about the net, and Shackle even more graceful and brilliant than Verriker, who was to sign with Boston and become a star in the NHL.

Shackle never got that chance.

The European IIHF maintained that he was the instigator, saying he had slashed the Soviet. So there was an uproar on both sides over it.

Verriker had jumped back over the boards to skate to his friend's assistance. And then he threw his stick at the referee and was expelled from the game. Another Canadian player tried to attack the Soviet bench as Shackle lay on the ice.

Yet the investigation which was started by the International Ice Hockey Federation dragged on and petered out. The Canadian hockey federation keyed it down. And after a run of time it seemed that nothing could be or would be done about it. It was a game Canada, playing mostly with university students, lost 5–3.

When Garth came home Vicki ran towards him. Pumpkin knew this as well. Vicki had read a romantic novel about a wounded man coming home after the Civil War and his love rushing into his arms and this was the posture she haltingly attempted. Yet at that moment there was a false note about her. Garth could not help but detect it.

She smiled but her face had a look of guilty shame on it – a look no one else would detect and he himself could never forget. Although she had cared nothing about hockey, she realized at that moment that the thousands in their grasp was gone forever, and this is what the look said.

Pumpkin was to see her mother's look of guilty shame many times over the years. And she was to know about both her mother's sadness and wonder. She was to see this look of guilty shame most particularly one night seven years ago in 1987, when Vicki was going to university, and was living on her own. It was a look Vicki could never hide from those closest to her.

It was now seven-thirty in the morning, and Pumpkin was just about done with her chores. The big black stud paced about in its own steam in the small paddock. The mare had walked with her colt down to the scraggly trees near the fence.

In the barn, Pumpkin was checking a rat trap near the

feed door, and for the last half-hour, Hector Wheem sat on a bale of hay watching her.

The boy and she had been inseparable for the last five years, ever since he and his mother, Jenna, had come to Taylorville.

Hector was the son of the professor, Christopher Wheem. Pumpkin knew this, though no one mentioned it more than once. As if it didn't matter, or as if it were something you only had to be told once.

The boy and his mother had found their way here to Taylorville. They had arrived one night, the boy bundled up in a snowsuit, the mother trying to handle four suit-cases and a large trunk. They had arrived at the small train station in the bitter snow, and were picked up in a car and driven away by one of Jenna Wheem's brothers. He was a small man with a pockmarked face and a huge beer gut. He was not a part of the story that Pumpkin knew.

He was Jenna Wheem's oldest brother, who could never leave her when she had nowhere else to go.

The boy had Down's syndrome, and most days and nights was at the Shackle barn. In fact, he had become to Pumpkin much like a brother, and to Garth a son.

"Hecksy – you're up some early today," she said.

The barn was gloomy and settled. The snow was still up past the plastic covering on the windows.

"Hecksy," Pumpkin said. "Where in hell is Louis today – have you seen Louis?"

Hector shook his head, but never broke his irrepress-ible grin.

Pumpkin had hired Louis Gatineau, a young Indian man, to help her because Garth was now too ill to walk any great distance.

But she had done the mucking out for the last two days. Louis might show up one day and not show up the next. Sometimes he would walk about the place as if he was bored and had nothing to do. He would kick things, like pails and buckets, out of his way. He always looked hurt and wronged about something whenever she looked his way.

He had said last week that he didn't make enough money.

So Pumpkin had offered him thirty cents more an hour.

But Louis had hummed and hawed about this. And he smoked in the barn.

"Garth better not catch you smoking in the barn," Pumpkin scolded. But she didn't have anyone else to help her, and so she didn't want to boss or scold him too much.

Last week too he had told Pumpkin that she had given them all smallpox. That it was her people. He liked to torment her with these stories as she worked. He told her that the governor had given his tribe blankets with smallpox germs and wiped out his entire civilization. That the governor had wanted to do this, and had had a great laugh, and took it as a big joke and that if she had read the right history she would know of this.

"What governor? I don't know any governor," Pumpkin had said.

He had added, lighting a cigarette, that when he was a little boy his grandmother had told him of the swamp measles. The whites had given them all heaps of German swamp measles. That's something else she didn't know.

Louis was twenty-one and lived on the reserve in a small trailer. His father, Sylvain Gatineau, used to beat him unmercifully, and had died drinking Lysol.

Louis had told her that one day he would drink Lysol. He had sniffed gasoline one time at the barn. She knew this but pretended she hadn't seen it.

He was okay with horses, but was fearful of the great stud.

Yesterday he had asked for money to go and see his sick grandmother for Easter. Pumpkin had gone into her savings, and had given him thirty extra dollars to take the train.

She had had to hide her money from her mother in an oat barrel, or her mother, who played the poker machines every day, would steal it.

Louis took the money, sniffed as if angry, walked across the snowy paddock in his cowboy boots.

"See you, Louis," she had called after him yesterday. "See you, okay?"

But by last night he was drunk.

He had not come to work today.

As always she was alone.

Pumpkin left Hector and walked back to the house. It was now light, and the dog followed her. She sighed as she went into the porch. Too many years. Too many years had passed. Now, it seemed, she knew too much. Too much about her mother that she did not want to know.

At the Shackle house on Holy Thursday, things were like this: her grandfather, Tom, had gone into the nearest big town to get the bus. He was going over to the university to get her Uncle Neil. For a number of years Neil had not come home. Phoning seemed useless. So old Tom decided to take the bus. Because Garth, who refused a doctor, was dying. Sometimes he spat up blood, or crawled on his belly to the toilet.

The snow had not stopped. The spruces took on the appearance they always had when clouds hung down; that is, they seemed heavy and far away. The road, cut off from half the world between the villages of Taylorville and Brickton, sat narrow and lonely. A horse had been brought across it an hour ago, hauling a sleigh filled with wood and boughs. In the distance there were ski slopes for the other people.

Inside the house were three people. Pumpkin, who had just come from the barn and had gone to her room.

Garth, lying in bed across the hallway from Pumpkin's room, had finally gone to sleep at five in the morning.

As the snow fell, Vicki, downstairs in the kitchen, sighed under her breath, and bit into a piece of toast. Garth had stopped speaking to her because she had desperately tried to contact his old hockey friend

Verriker for money last week. "Just a few thousand," she had said.

The early morning, the sound of her sighs, the crunching of toast seemed to attest to this new falling out between them. And now Vicki, who had been out half the night, was preparing to go out again. She had finally got the car started, and Pumpkin could hear it idling, almost stalling out every ten seconds.

Late last night Garth had told Pumpkin to go away.

"Go away – get out of here – get on the train before you get hurt. I made plans for you to go to Vancouver so why are you waiting here?" he had said, staring wildly at her, "I'm all right –"

"I'm not going –" Pumpkin had whispered, taking out a white morphine tablet. She had tried to stuff it into his mouth as he tried to bite her finger.

She had sat with him most of the night, had helped him down the hall to the toilet.

At four this morning he had asked for Neil. So little Pumpkin knew the end was near.

"Where in hell," he said, quite gently, "is my brother Neil? Is he still at university? Professor Neil Shackle – he has been away from us so long."

It was a truth Pumpkin no longer had to be told.

It was Holy Thursday, at seven-forty-five in the morning. When Neil Shackle woke he could see through the bedroom window the streetlight at the corner, and a pitiless snowbank. The trees were still, while snow was beginning to fall in tiny mean flakes.

He let Anna sleep, and went for a moment into his study. He turned on the radio. Neil's radio was always tuned to the CBC. And although Neil at one time would have recognized its patronizing parental attitude, he no longer did. He now felt comfortable with the way everything was being said and discussed.

He did not recognize many things about himself that had changed, which anyone from his family or his town would.

Why would his father come today? Thinking of this fact – that his father was travelling on a bus to see him – made him worry. Perhaps there was a terrible thing happening at home. That is, perhaps it wasn't just because Garth was ill.

He sat at the desk and turned on the study lamp, and looked at the pages of an article he had been writing for a scholarly journal, on how the quota system might or might not work in a certain way within a given set of circumstances.

At the heart of his article was the idea that a plan could be applied that would give the victim a chance. Except somewhere within this article he had lost track of who the victim was and how to rectify the abuse of one set or group of people without scapegoating another. This was the main problem of his article. It was what he was taking pains to try to clarify, before he had to send the article away.

He had promised to send it away before Easter. He had started it with much enthusiasm, but had put it aside so often he wasn't even sure now if he wanted to finish it.

He stood, turned off the study lamp, and left the room.


Neil had lived in this university town for twenty-five years.

He had come from Taylorville in the late 1960s.

He had come from a spot on the map with nine houses and one road, cut off from the world by a suicidal turn that was unpaved. He never forgot this.

He never forgot that he would meet a boy from small-town Ontario who was to have a particular contempt for him, and for his family, and by this contempt make his life miserable for a number of years; and that he would meet another boy, who would actually revere his family more than he himself was able to.

That he would meet both at this small battered university in 1968.

One was a nineteen-year-old Ontario boy named Christopher Wheem.

Wheem continually looked at Neil, with something born out of injured merit, belief in his own superiority, resentment at being cast down into a howling Maritime pit.

He was, Neil now supposed, in some ways right.

It started to snow early here; the ground froze solid. The darkness came with small forlorn streetlights punctuating the flinty evening. The houses were wooden and faded.

Professors did not travel much past the outskirts of the city. Most longed to be somewhere else. Most pretended they were. By early autumn the sky was as grey as aluminum siding. The smell of wood smoke rose up against the great cliffs to the east.

The mining operation nearby had sunk itself into nothing, and nothing else existed except the tire plant and the university.

The roads were battered and raw; the whole place woods and water. By early November they were trudging to class through the Homeric leaves, in the snow. The university looked northern in its base brick and glass buildings strewn about the unlevel campus. And Wheem hated it, and anyone like Neil Shackle, who might remind him of where he was.

The British professors followed soccer, the Americans existed on baseball. Everyone pretended they had never left home. Everyone pretended something or other.

And so Wheem pretended too. Neil now supposed it was the only way he had found to exist. He told everyone that he was a Philosophy major and that his father owned a great business somewhere in Ontario. But then someone who knew his family, who came one miserable night from the other provincial university, told people this was not true, that Wheem's father was a failed insurance broker; his mother belonged to a bowling team called the Silver Sisters. This was all so long ago – in 1968.

In 1968 Neil also met Anna Bracken, who was to become his wife – in the commonlaw sense.

He had known her as a girl from his neighbouring village of Brickton. She was a shy, kindly girl with a broad forehead, and her long hair was pinned back, so that her ears showed. He began to date her in the fall of that year.

All of this was now a memory this Holy Thursday, as vivid as painful memories tend to be.

One November night he had brought Anna through the side door and into the smoky lobby of Dr. Knowles's Residence, before they went to a little theatre that ran movies at that time only on weekends, and then only with re-runs from fifteen years before, punctuated always by faulty change-overs and missing reels.

Wheem was sitting in the lobby of the residence – named after a biochemist from the 1930s. He watched Anna come in, and then, looking at his friend Bobby Coner, he made a comment out of the side of his mouth that was at once cheapened by his smile.

But Wheem's friend, noticing the girl was lame,

acknowledged this lameness, in an expression of wondrous and humble sympathy.

The movie that night was terrible – the silent ancient ticket-taker in his grey suit escorting them with a flashlight to a row of empty seats, amongst rows of other empty seats.

Neil held Anna's hand for the first time, and learned that she had been a friend of Vicki, his sister-in-law. He wondered now this Holy Thursday why he didn't understand something of it then – of Vicki's envy. That is, her envy of Anna.

But this was so, so long ago – in 1968.

Wheem came to Neil's room a few nights after the movie.

It was a cold night, in late November, and there was something sterile in the smell of the hall, in the look of the scratched telephone near the proctor's door. The trees tapped away, at nothing, the last frozen leaves curled like small bats hanging dead on the crooked branches.

Wheem paced up and down the room so his shadow was cut in two by Neil's blinds.

He asked about Neil's brother Garth – was he really a hockey player who'd married a gorgeous beauty? He asked about Anna – how did Neil ever manage to attract such an attractive woman?

But then Wheem became serious. The entire thing was perhaps posture, Neil thought now. Wheem said he had come to offer advice. He wore a small stud in his ear, and had on his green silk shirt. He was so much a product of the new world – the world encroaching on them – the world that lay across an abyss and which Neil wanted to be a part of.

Wheem looked at the small black-and-white picture of Neil's mother and father, and then, looking sad, he took Anna's picture in his thin, long hands.

"Hey," he said with quiet emotion, as he set the picture down, "you don't want Anna to end up like your mother – I hope she doesn't end up bred and barefoot at nineteen. You don't want this, Neil, do you?"

Another picture showed Neil's tiny mother standing by a tumbledown shed at the back of their house, in the long hay in July 1953 with a silver-sided covered bridge in the distance.

"Just be careful," Wheem said. "Be careful how you treat her. I know how people like you think – I mean way up in that . . . place, and having all those kids. Let me tell you there are others of us who don't take kindly to that thing any more."

Wheem rubbed his reddened thumb as if he was distressed because his thumb was sore. And then he turned to Neil and smiled unnaturally. Perhaps filled with the kind of ego that marked his life he was unsure of why he had said what he had.

Just then something else happened. Neil's brother Reggie, whom Neil had not seen in three years, came into the room. He had been in Gagetown training recruits in artillery fire. He was dressed in his brown uniform and wore black army boots.

"So this is where you are – I been lookin all over –"
he said.

Neil was too surprised to say or do anything.

Wheem nodded, and left the room quickly, preoccupied with rubbing his thumb.

Neil sat down and smoothed the bed with his short stubby fingers. He tried to be pleasant, but Reggie's huge uncouth appearance upset him. If Reggie had not come in he would have hit Wheem for his family's sake, and yet he was embarrassed by his brother. Reggie knew this. Neil was embarrassed by everything, by his own life, and hope. Reggie, holding a care package for him, sensed this too.

This was the first time Neil had ever been annoyed with anyone in his family for being who they were. He wanted Reggie to go away and leave him alone. Reggie, who used to carry him home on his shoulders from sliding while he tapped a tune on Reggie's big head.

Reggie, who had not got out of grade ten and had joined the army.

Reggie, who had a mark across his neck from being caught in the traces of their draft horse, Timothy. Reggie, who had once met the premier.

Reggie, who had fought a forest fire to the foot of the Gratten family's door, refusing to abandon their house even after the family had all run away.

Neil remembered his brother Reggie now this Holy Thursday, and that incident with painful clarity.

At the University that first year there was another boy

who knew Garth and Vicki, Tom, and Neil's mother, Dorothy. Who knew the history of the reserve across the river and St. Brenden's Church.

Emile Dexter, Anna's cousin, was now dead. He had been a friend of Garth's, his best man, and had played hockey with him. He'd come to their house dozens of times. He too was from Taylorville. And he was on a small scholarship.

You do not always know how things happen. They just do, and then in hindsight and with reflection, you have the feeling of an epiphany – of some kind of justice in the faintest measure in all things, all events. And this is what Neil felt now.

One night, just before Christmas of that year, Dexter had threatened Wheem in his room, and told him to leave people alone or he would be sorry. That someday all of his guile would come back upon him.

From that moment Wheem was ingratiating to Dexter's face, and loathed him behind his back. But Dexter's threat also caused Wheem to become kinder to Neil and to Anna.

There was some talk that this incident between Dexter and Wheem had occurred because Wheem was making fun of Anna and of Neil's family, but Neil did not hear of this until much later, until Dexter had left the university.

Anna had been drinking the night before. And she had said something to him. She had finally said what she had been thinking for years, that he had never been Dexter's friend, although when certain benefits arose from being a friend of a writer he postured as one.

She made accusations now and again, and he was often hurt by them. And he would give a touching grimace when she said something, and he wouldn't answer. Yet last night he'd tried to defend himself.

He said that Dexter was always out of control. He had threatened Wheem. He drank too much, and people knew this would be the end of him. And this is what he really did die of – drink – didn't he?

"And far be it from you to threaten Wheem, or anyone," Anna retorted.

Neil thought of Anna this morning. He was trying to remember how many drinks she had had the night before.

Their life had started out lightheartedly – years and years ago. They both believed in justice and fairness, and kindness.

He turned at the bottom of the stairs and went into the kitchen, which because of the early hour of the morning gave a spiteful unlived feeling. Sebastian the cat lay across the table, and looked at him without purring.

He thought of what his life had been like for twenty-five years. He did not exonerate himself by this process. He knew how much he had hated his youth and where he had come from; how much he wanted to cross that abyss to the world in which Wheem hovered.

And he thought of C.S. Lewis's inner circle, and how he too wanted to belong.

During the first few months at university Neil mentioned with much affection his brother Garth, his father, Tom, and his oldest brother, Reggie. He spoke about his mother's death. But as time went on, he felt less and less inclined to. And sometimes, when people from away, from that new world which he needed to belong to, spoke about "those" people, which in essence meant his people, and what they must be like, Neil would remain silent. He thought he would mention them – sometime down the road. That sometime when it was right to do so he would. And now and again, he felt himself looking back at the abyss that separated his new world from his old. An abyss he was struggling across and which he thought he was the only one to know.

One night, they sat in Coner's room at the back end of the hall. Snow was coming down outside. It was mid-winter.

Wheem was always the first to do anything. And now he showed them a manuscript of a story he was writing. He asked them if they would like to hear it, and when no one said anything one way or the other he began to read.

It was a story about an unhappy aristocratic woman from Ontario married to a balding senator – a Canadian senator (which to Wheem seemed to be exactly like an American senator). In this crude story, Wheem made a great deal of this senator's terrible physical shape and right-wing sentiments, and howled and laughed as he read. Outside, the night had frozen up all the doors and windows, and snow drifted across the empty parking lots.

The senator's wife ended up having a liberating affair with a student much like Wheem. The sexual prowess of the young man was laboured over and discussed in detail – this seemed to be the most serious part of the text.

Wheem finally put the manuscript aside, lit a cigarette, and blew smoke into the room. But no one said anything. A few people grinned.

Wheem then said he would become a professor and write a novel. Neil said nothing. He only smiled when Wheem glanced at him. He had seen the same story at the movie theatre, three months before.

"I'm immensely European," Wheem said, fondling the manuscript and showing the smile he always showed when he was trying to be liked.

Coner laughed, but didn't know why.

One of the Indian boys, Peter Bathurst, from the reserve said: "You come back to my reserve an I'll tell you a story." And then he looked at Neil and winked.

And Wheem smiled. He enjoyed the attention and it seemed this was the main point of his exercise. He said he didn't need to know much about woodlots, or hockey – and here he glanced Neil's way. But people could see he was defensive and no one wanted to mention anything else about it.

"Well, I don't know much about it," Dexter, who had been in the room, said finally, "so I wish you luck."

Wheem looked over at him, nodded and frowned.

By this time of year there was that disturbing smell of dark salt in the snow. The windows were always frozen shut. The dormitories looked like prisoner's cells. And the days went on, frigid and endless.

Coner would come over to Neil's room and they would talk. One night, about a week after Wheem read his story, Coner whispered into the dark, still air, while he smoked his cigarette: "Wheem says this is the age of women – only men like Wheem would connive to use it to their advantage. Listen to his story about the aristocratic woman and know he knows nothing about anything. Don't get me wrong. Wheem is bright, very, very bright, in a crafty way. He will always get along – in everything. He will cross the stream into the new world. But Dexter is the man."

"Dexter," Neil said, whispering laughter back across the black room.

"Dexter," Coner said, whispering into the blue cold, and rubbing the toes on his left foot. "Dexter, however, will not get along – even his friends will curse him. He will never be able to cross. He will die before he does."

Often when Coner was visiting, Wheem would come to the door and smile in at them, as if trying to reassert himself.

Neil and Anna moved into an apartment. He got his B.A. that spring. For a few years Wheem hung about with a different crowd. He was president of Students for a Democratic Solution, and would appear on cable TV in a poncho, talking about Bakunin.

Dexter stayed in university, tried to make it in Arts, but finally quit after he lost his scholarship and went back home to work. Peter Bathurst went back to the reserve, and for a while was put in jail for a fight.

One time in the autumn of 1972 Neil received a phone call from the bus depot. He went down to retrieve a package.

It was twelve jars of preserves from home, in an old Zeller's box, which his father, Tom, had sent him with a note about the family. He and Anna joined the Film Society when Tom was in the hospital with a cracked disc in his back he had suffered while lifting an engine housing.

They took walks along the green, admired crafts in the sun-drenched windows, and listened to the latest announcers on CBC describe how horrified they were by violence, when Reggie was in the Gaza Strip.

Anna's lameness gave everything they did a certain poignancy and character, which was intrinsically a part of their studies and their quiet married life. That she had a certain amount of money that had fallen from her father's fallen grace seemed to add to this. So too did the fact that they lived near a university.

Neil handled her money carefully, even meticulously. But when she mentioned this to him he would say: "Yes, well, you haven't grown up like I have, have you – if you grew up like that – well, maybe you would be more careful as well."

For a few years Neil travelled back and forth from his future into his past and back again. He would help each

July with his father's haying, and go and help with the horses. But there were always arguments, and Neil could not seem to help it.

Neil had turned into "some kind of an atheist," his father thought, since he didn't have a church wedding, and his father would tell him he should go to church and pray, and that they had some genuine saints' bones in the vestry.

Neil had forgotten some of the reasons things were said or done at home. He tried at times to graft the new world to the old and found it could not be grafted.

All of this was long, long ago.

Garth and Vicki would sometimes make the pilgrimage over to see them. Neil remembered this now this Holy Thursday when things were so difficult for them. He remembered not only Vicki's beauty, but her sad envy, her longing to have things that she and Garth just did not have.

And would never have.

Neil tried to write a book about his past, yet he found himself unable to tell the truth in this book, and he would always put it off. His world was no longer the world of his brothers and so he found it hard to talk of his love for them. That he still loved them was true; that he was always apologizing for them was true as well.

Because he couldn't write exactly what he wanted to, he started to write a futuristic novel, about a contest of wills between an artist and a biochemist. Everyone said it was fun to listen to, a gas when he read it to some friends, because Neil knew chemistry very well.

In his novel art was banned, chemistry had become religion and religion had created mutants. Everyone in his group praised it, but it was never published, and eventually forgotten.

By 1975 almost everyone in the little group he knew was trying to write a book of some kind – or was an artist of some kind. Everyone considered themselves friends.

Almost everyone he knew from his former life would think of these people as absurdly self-centred and neurotic.

He met Wheem again, at the small writing club they had. Wheem was writing angrily now about the CIA. Therefore he thought he was writing a novel infused with intrigue and danger.

The winters came and they stayed inside, together. Outside the snow fell. It fell over the scraggly trees that sat upon the cliffs to the east. It fell over the empty mine pits, the headframes of a desolate shaft, the fields of pit-props.

It fell against the red brick buildings, and small windows of classrooms and offices.

It fell over the cliffs, the dozens of small bungalows where people from town who worked in the tire plant lived.

Neil, finishing his Master's, wearing his light tweeds and heavy shoes, which gave him a youthful apprentice look, was fairly well liked in the university group back then.

He forgot about home – where he had come from – for months on end. He forgot about Garth and Vicki, and sometimes from somewhere especially far away he would get a note from Reggie; Reggie, the picture of a sand dune, the middle of a desert.

"I lost my camel," Reggie would write in an amusing note. He would ask them to look up two people – Gretta Bartibog, and her daughter, whose name he thought was Diane.

Neil knew that Diane Bartibog – the little girl who sometimes came to the house when he was a boy – was Reggie's daughter. But it was one of those private family matters; matters that were not mentioned.

Then something happened. In 1976 something happened that those who had long been at the centre of the artistic community that Neil was so proud to belong to hadn't predicted.

A young writer came out of nowhere, and would publish three books in the course of the next seven years. Books about the very place Neil grew up – books about his people and town. Books about people like Peter Bathurst and men like Reggie Shackle.

This young writer was outside of all groups and made all groups jealous – each in their own way. Even Neil, though he wouldn't admit it.

This writer was Emile Dexter.

That autumn of 1976, when Dexter published his first

book, Neil became depressed. Certain phrases came to him that Dexter had once said, and that Neil hadn't realized were important.

The phrases, the remarks, now seemed to drift in the air like snowflakes tinged with smoke over the cliffs and headframes, and down across Dr Knowles's Residence.

The remarks reminded him of a plea for and a recrimination about the other world – the old age that was disappearing and was being replaced by new-wave discos and shopping malls. And Neil was angry that he had not recognized this in Dexter before or had not tried to defend this world himself.

Now he realized how separated he had become from this world by the mid-1970s and how it was fruitless to try to fathom why.

On the day Dexter's first book was launched, Wheem married Jenna Pottier in a small country church. It was raining, the wind blew the outside tables over.

Wheem had found no one to be best man, and phoned to ask Neil the night before the wedding.

And so time passed on. And things pretty well returned to normal at university. Dexter's book was not lauded in the important papers. A few students carried it about. And it had a certain following. But little by little it was forgotten.

After a number of months Wheem's dislike of Dexter had returned and that, too, was normal.

When people spoke of Dexter, Wheem would recount how Dexter had threatened him. He would look at Neil and then say: "A clever writer – in a certain way – but a horrible man." He always said this in front of women because Wheem knew intellectual women were the first to become offended by Dexter's treatment of female characters.

By this time, about 1977, Neil found himself fully entrenched in a world his father and his brothers would not understand. And therefore in many ways he found that he did not understand them.

In the fall of 1977 a new writer-in-residence came to the university. And the woman came to the job with great enthusiasm. Neil told Anna about her. He himself treated her with great respect, read her one book – about a single mother and the tragedy of a single mother's life – and felt fortunate to have helped her settle. It was a duty and function of the university that he do this, and it made him especially proud.

The writer wanted a Maritime setting and Neil found a place near the stream a mile from the university. However, she was neurotic about noise, and there was a gravel pit nearby, near those terrible dark cliffs.

She was no more than settled when she asked him to move her again. He complied. And never a day went by when there wasn't some complaint filed with him about some crisis: the sun was in her eyes where she worked; her writing students hadn't read all of a certain writer she admired; her office was too cramped.

Neil scurried about trying to help her as much as he

could. She left notes in his box continually, which Neil felt special to receive. It was annoying to receive them but he would not want to give up his obligation.

Neil was always allowing himself tongue-lashings from her because she was known as a very famous Canadian author.

She sipped sherry and was always convalescing. The snow fell and fell, the mine shaft looked broken and damp.

From home that year there was an attack on Dexter, and his book. The attack went like this: he was wealthy, and wrote about "poor people," which gave his province, already struggling against this fierce stereotype, a worse reputation than it deserved. Certain of the university staff picked up on this criticism as well.

Neil was working on his doctorate, and didn't have time to read Dexter at that moment or to take part in the controversy, even though others believed he could because of his brilliant understanding of the Maritimes and his own poor background.

After a time Neil found that his presence could bring looks of sympathy and understanding from compassion-ate outsiders, because of how they felt about Dexter maligning the poor of the province.

And though Neil tried to remain neutral he found himself succumbing to this critical posture.

To Neil, there was the rueful comfort in the safety and warmth of the university. He became somewhat the centre of attention. Coming from the same small area of the province he became Dexter's opposite voice. And this gave him a kind of odd intellectual power. He knew it and he suspected Dexter knew it also.

He tried to fight this, but so many people loved him he could not fight it well. In fact he tried for a while to play both sides and found it impossible.

And time marched on.

"The professors prefer Wheem," the writer-in-residence said one glowing winter afternoon to Neil, as they each had a glass of sherry, which showed she was privy to the most sensitive information.

She spoke with a tremendous sympathy in her voice for Wheem, who, she felt, was being maligned. "And the greatest writer of us all."

Secretly it felt very gratifying not to be Dexter at this time, so Neil said nothing. And Wheem did look hurt.

He looked at Neil as if Neil should come on-side as well, and say what everyone else in the department now said about his CIA novel: "That, in a certain way, Wheem was better."

Neil did not know what this certain way was.

But he slowly realized that Wheem could be more important a writer than Dexter if the others, at the centre of the artistic circle here, decided he was.

But as always, always, his family was to come back to haunt him, and though he still loved them, he felt far removed in time and place from them. From the smell of the barn and the rats in the horse feed.

In February 1978, Garth came to see him. There was a gentle snow falling outside the windows of his and Anna's blackened brick apartment on Fedder Lane. This was a lane in the back of town, in between the two cliffs, with the university on one side and the hospital on the other. There were hardly any streetlights on this lane, but Neil and Anna could hear Garth's old car a long way away.

Garth and Vicki came to the door with two small suitcases, with their daughter trailing behind.

Twilight ran thinly against the shelves of books, the small cups and saucers, the plain stark windows that Anna had decorated with homemade curtains. Looking outside, you might have been in any small Maritime community – or in any in northern Ontario.

Garth was nervous, like a huge child. He had not known Neil well, and had not seen him in a few years. Neil was clumsily trying to act natural. He had not been home in so long.

Garth's nose was bent, his back was slanted to the right, and he had long ago lost his teeth. When he smiled he showed his gums. Of course he still had some bottom teeth, and he had a plate which he refused to wear. He took pills to ease the pain in his left shoulder. His heart had been bruised.

He would often travel about the province to attend sports functions in honour of other people – actually, in honour of people who had made it to the NHL, or into the Sports Hall of Fame.

"Someday I'll get there," he sniffed, after he told Neil about going to a Hall of Fame dinner.

Every time he opened his mouth Vicki would say: "Now, Garth – now, Garth."

He walked with a noticeable limp. It was also noticeable how distressed Vicki was over this limp. They sat down after supper in the crowded living room, to talk. They talked for an hour or two, almost always in a kind of mumble. Just once Garth mentioned *the* game, and how he never saw the check.

Neil had hated hockey since he was a child anyway, perhaps because Garth had been the favourite child, the one the family had such hopes for. He stared out the window, at the snow that fell. Now and then he glanced sideways at Vicki, who glanced at him and then shifted those beautiful eyes. Now and again little Pumpkin would cough, grab a Kleenex and blow her nose.

"Scuse me."

"Blow yer nose – blow blow blow blow," Vicki would say. "Don't sniff it up – blow it all out."

"Now what's that – some big guitar?" Garth asked about the cello.

"No, that's a cello."

"Ah ya – I heard you played on that," Garth said.

The wind began to blow, the way it did on the day of Garth and Vicki's wedding ten years before, when everything was possible for them. When the world was theirs. When Garth still lived everyone's dream.

Vicki kept looking here and there. She wore a tight yellow skirt and a large-sleeved blouse, a small necklace, and the huge diamond which Garth had got her when she was nineteen that seemed to take up her entire finger.

She had been mistaken at a truckstop one day for a prostitute when she and Garth were on the road, and Neil, seeing her skirt and makeup, now realized how this could have happened.

Every time Vicki made a mistake in grammar she corrected herself and looked sheepishly at Anna, whose life she always secretly envied, and whom she made fun of.

And finally their question was posed.

They wanted Neil to loan them money for a little bar and tavern they wanted to open next to the reserve. They had no credit, and Vicki's father had turned his back on them. Tom had no real capital, and Garth and Vicki were in a bind.

It took them three hours to ask this favour, and both burst out laughing when they did. They were so intimidated by Neil, and he had never known it.

"We don't want to go to Mickey Dunn," Vicki said. "We want to play disco music – it's what all the kids love now – not like us, Neil, eh?"

Neil remembered once before, when they visited, how Vicki couldn't stop talking about Mickey Dunn; how he had been a godsend for them. How he helped them both when Garth first came home. But now, as if she were relating knowledge Neil would be secretly impressed by, she kept saying: "You don't know Mickey like I know Mickey

– Garth – Garth, he don't know Mickey like I know Mickey – Mickey runs everything – he'd do anything for us – you have to be careful with Mickey – I know Mickey."

Their child, Penny, or Pumpkin, as everyone except his wife Anna called her, sat in a chair near the window, in a thin dress, reminding Neil of some drab painting from the 1940s.

The wind blew again; the sign across the street flickered numbly.

It was the only time Garth had ever asked Neil for anything. Anything at all, and Neil could not help. He did not want to give the money he had carefully saved and invested from Anna's small endowment for a bar, or put his credit on the line by a counter-signature, because he was still unsure of his tenure. It had taken him eight years to save this money, to put it into a small investment where the return was humble.

He explained this. It took him forty minutes to do so. Anna interrupted him many times but he knew his concern was correct.

Pumpkin, who hadn't understood what had been said, blurted: "I knew you would help us, cause Mommie always said you were the best to us!"

And she looked about, smiling. It was as if she had prepared this statement on the way over in the car, and was damned if she wasn't going to say it.

Neil asked them to wait another year or two and then they would gladly help. But this wasn't what they wanted to hear.

"Well, you made it, Neil – that's one of us, anyways," Garth said.

Neil flinched and nodded. He had saved Anna's little endowment well. He had not given into temptation and bought the paintings he wanted.

Of course he had never written the book that he wanted to either, never stood in line in front of opposing armies like Reggie, and never suffered on the ice for his country.

Vicki sat in the chair staring at him. She was smiling as if she really wanted to like him. Now, years later, on Holy Thursday, he thought of her stare, her full beauty at twenty-eight years old, and a twinge of horrifying guilt overcame him. It was as if at that moment he had condemned her to an agony, and a death.

She smiled so beautifully. It was all she could do.


Dexter visited Neil only once. It was a quiet night in the middle of spring in 1980, a year after the second book was published. It was a book about a failed hockey player and his wife.

It hadn't sold well, and Dexter said he didn't think he would ever write any more.

"That's too bad," Neil said, although secretly he was glad. But this was not what Dexter had come to say. Writing, he said, was simply a mistake.

Dexter had actually come to find out if they knew that the bar was lost. The hopes of Neil's sister-in-law dashed. That they had owed Mickey Dunn fourteen rotten thousand dollars from the loan – and because of this, Mickey had taken control of the entire little bar and tavern, near the reserve, which they were once so proud of. That everyone felt this would happen and that Vicki was not well liked anymore. Not in Taylorville – not any-place else.

"I see," Neil said. He felt angry at this interference in his family's affairs. He felt angered by this non-judge-mental, knowledgeable intrusion. He felt angry over the book as well. A book he had not yet read but whose con-tents he'd been told about. Yet Dexter had not consciously written about Garth or Vicki. It was simply that every-thing he had written seemed to Neil to have a link with Garth's world.

And though Neil had lost contact with that world, he still saw it every day. He saw it in Anna's smile, and in the accents of his hopeful young students, who'd come down to him from the north or up from the small towns in the south.

It was in their world where Dexter had placed his hockey player, and his hockey player's doomed self-serving wife.

While Dexter was there Anna was out shopping. Neil had never really known how to entertain anyone without her, and there was a terrible pause; Dexter looked about and smiled.

Neil would be on a salary for life. He would have stu-dents, comfort, and poetry. "But Dexter is the man," he remembered Bobby Coner's voice from years ago. The only serious comment Bobby Coner ever made. And he thought of Bobby Coner, his loud music in a room constantly filled with the stench of marijuana, his lumpy socks, his flat shoes, and how he stared goggle-eyed at Anna, in wondrous sympathy.

Neil went over to see his father that July. He decided during a day in the hayfield to see the tavern at some point. To see what all the fuss was about. Garth and Vicki were away.

It felt good to be in the hayfield again. The day was hot. Across the river the reserve sat blinded in the heat. The slanted roofs, the smoke from the far-off dump. A dry road led through its centre, and now and then a car silently travelled that road.

In the late afternoon he went down to the river to sit and drink a bottle of beer. A salmon rolled in the rip just out from him.

He looked at the reserve indifferently. He had not been over there in a long time. He used to go over and play with Peter Bathurst when he was a child. Now, in the heat of midsummer, with his pants wet and his arms scratched by the bales of hay, he realized that twenty years had passed since then.

The young Diane Bartibog used to tag along with them. A lanky youngster with wobbly knees and a big smile. He knew even then that she was Reggie's daughter. That was the secret the family – his family – had always tried to hide. It was also the reason for Reggie's leaving home and going into the army.

He remembered that Reggie had beaten three men at the garage because they had made fun of Gretta Bartibog.

Sitting there at the river's edge all those years later, it was as if a door had suddenly opened that allowed him to see clearly into his past world, to notice little Diane Bartibog's wondrous, wondrous smile. He tried to retain the feeling this gave him, and stared at the label on the bottle of Moosehead Ale, as if to encourage this feeling not to pass. But soon the feeling, like the smoke from the distant dump, drifted away.

Garth and Vicki were out of town, on another meaningless errand for Mickey Dunn, so Neil walked across the bridge that night, thinking that he would ask Mickey Dunn about the control he exercised over his family.

But when he got to the bar Mickey was not there.

He tried to think of all the things he might have done in his life if he had stayed here. He would certainly have worked at the mill in Brickton, married someone else, curled at the small curling rink in the winter.

As he sat sipping an ale, with the jukebox playing a Merle Haggard tune, feeling his muscles ache for the first time in years, his fingers blistered, he was mistaken for his brother Reggie. At first it didn't seem important, yet Neil was no match for the two men who came over to his table. And if truth be told he had always been protected by Reggie or by Garth. But now Reggie was in the army, and Garth was out of town.

A fear filled him at being mistaken for his brother, which was more pronounced because of the heat, the smell of frying onions and wieners. By the fact that his brothers were not here.

Neil had taken great pains all of his life not to be like Reggie, not to get mixed up on the reserve with Indian women – not to fight.

"Sorry – I'm Neil," he said firmly.

"No sorry," Sylvain Gatineau said. "I see you, Reggie – somp time pretty soon – I get you dere for makin bad of me." And he held up his fist. He had a tattoo on the underside of his arm. His face was brown and flinty.

Neil did not know Sylvain well. He had heard he had a little boy, Louis, whom he mistreated, betting money by forcing him to eat sour pickles, and that he had stabbed a man in a drunken brawl over a comb.

There were things done which were horrible, and Neil knew this. He knew this, but he no longer understood it. So Neil became frightened, and in his fear he got up and left the bar, hearing laughter behind him.

He realized he had thrown his relatives into danger. For if they thought *Reggie* had turned from them, what would they now think of Tom or Garth? How could Garth protect himself now?

He wanted to go back and confront them. But he couldn't bring himself to go back into the bar. Finally he went home. His father greeted him happily at the door because he had come up from the university to help with the hay. His father wanted to sit in the kitchen and talk about a new mare he was going to buy.

Neil talked, but his heart wasn't in it. It wasn't in the

new mare, or the smell of manure in the soft night air. He saw his father, his left hand missing a thumb, his old workshirt with a pack of Export makings in it. He felt sick at heart and walked upstairs.

The room was small and cramped. The old homemade bedspread, with its small cotton balls, irritated him because in it he saw the supreme gift of kindly innocence. Not only of his mother, but of his father.

The walls in this old room were slanted, a broken crucifix sat in one corner. A picture of Reggie when he was fifteen reining Timothy out of the back woodlot sat on the dresser covered with dust.

Neil sat on the edge of the bed for an hour, going over in his mind how to escape from the responsibility of his action at the bar.

It was a gentle night, a sweet midsummer night. Far across the bridge at the bar he could hear laughter again. The sounds and shouts of Indian women.

The people on the reserve had become more vocal about their treaty. They wanted to stop white people from fishing the tract just below his farm. Peter Bathurst wanted native self-government.

But Sylvain Gatineau's threat had nothing to do with that. Although that would be the pretence.

The secret was that he had sought to escape all of this when he left home some twelve years before. And he had, he had – he had almost managed it. But it, whatever it was, kept coming back.

He sat for a long time, trying to put some perspective

on this, on poor Vicki's failed dream, on Garth, whom he felt he had betrayed. He thought of how admirable it was for John Keats to send money to his brother George – how noble that act of self-denial was. He himself loved Keats, yet had not acted like that. He had saved his money. Kept it well away from others. He saw in the corner of the room the torn grey suitcase Vicki had carried when she had come to visit them, and was saddened.

He also thought, quite suddenly, of Peter Bathurst's little cousin, Gregory Pie, the one who froze to death in 1961.

They had all gone to the boy's home. The little body lay with its hands folded, in a small borrowed suit. The look on the face was one of a gentle plea, with his lips slightly turned down in a grimace. Sister St. Rita stood watching her students cross themselves. And Neil, looking at her blue hands, remembered how those hands had dragged little Gregory Pie out of the classroom the previous September, and how those hands had shaken him. And how he'd had on the same sweater his older brother had worn the year before, a blue sweater, with a tiny red patch near the heart.

They went to the funeral at St. Brenden's. The priest, who was well known to hate maudlin affairs, rushed the incense by the coffin. The candle flames fluttered and spit. The Virgin Mary looked down with quiet, sad eyes.

Peter Bathurst was sitting in the front pew. He turned to Neil and smiled, and said, quite foolishly: "He looked somp natty in that suit," and then began to cry.

Peter was ten then. He had tried to save his cousin, but hadn't been able to. Everyone said he was a hero for trying. He was perhaps going to become a great man.

Peter Bathurst had become a great man.

For the first time Neil felt he himself would not be.

Neil had sat on the bed thinking of this, and so many other things, on that night of July 29, 1980.

The rats had all gone. A certain level of security had come.

"You are called to do things and you must do them." This is what his reading of Cicero had told him. He had been called upon to help his brother, to loan his brother money, and he had not. And if he had done so two years ago everything would be different now. Dexter's second novel, the novel that Anna loved, that seemed to be in answer to Garth's plea for money, might not have been written.

Mickey Dunn might no longer control his brother and sister-in-law's terrible little lives. That they were terrible little lives there was no doubt.

And then he thought of Dexter's first novel, called *The Bald Hills*. That too was about his family in a way.

The novel was about a man like Neil, who must face who he is, or become forever a man like Wheem. The novel ended on a bus, the main character travelling at night.

Sitting on the edge of the bed he felt there was only one thing to do. He would prove them all wrong. He would go to Mickey Dunn. He was thinking of how he would confront Mickey about the shabby treatment of his family and how, suddenly, because of himself, it would all be resolved. Yet in his heart he only wanted Mickey Dunn to like him, and to realize that he was not like his brothers.

The next morning, he dressed and went to the bar early. It was gloomy and dark inside with the leftover scent of beer and pickled wieners. Outside was another hot day. There was the sound of machines and jackhammers at the site of the little mall they were starting to build.

Above old St. Brenden's, an empty lot had been bought by Peter Bathurst to build his house.

Neil sat in the office with its deep-brown leather chair, his hair neat and groomed.

Mickey was in the back room. When Mickey came out to meet him the idea was suddenly this: that there was no one in the world that Mickey respected or wanted to meet more than Neil Shackle. And Neil, in spite of himself – in spite of all that he wanted to say, had planned – felt greatly relieved.

Mickey easily confided in him. He told him not to mind Sylvain Gatineau. That he, Mickey, would take care of the problem. He also told Neil how much he respected the Shackle family. That in fact there was no other family on the river he respected more. He sucked some chocolate off his fingers as he looked forlornly about.

Mickey went on, his flat face looking genuinely hurt at something. He spoke about trying to protect Garth and Vicki from people who would take advantage of them.

That though he had "no education himself" and was "some stupid" compared to Neil and "all those other big wheels," he tried his best. He was always fair.

"I'm sorry if I sound stupid to you," he said.

"No no no no," Neil said, moving forward in his chair eagerly.

Neil tried to question him about Garth and Vicki in a way that showed he had mettle. And Mickey allowed this, studying him quietly, his eyes seeming nonchalantly vague, and then he said, "I love Garth and Vicki – Dr. Shackle. I'm here to handle their affairs. Here – come – cut my arm off if you think different." And he held out his short stocky arm, with the white mole, and smiled. Then he winked at him, and Neil felt genuinely moved.

Neil tried to continue asking questions about Garth, about the bar, about how much money Tom had to pay, but felt if he mentioned what he knew it would be indiscreet. Also, there was just a hint of a lie taking place. That is, everything that Dexter had said to Neil in confidence that night when he came to visit might be true, but, as a favour, Dunn was implicitly asking Neil to ignore it. That if he didn't mention it, things would go better for him.

Then Dunn mentioned Dexter. He looked at Neil squarely, and said: "I hope that's not the kind of writing that my kids have to read at university. Lies about his community. Everyone's up in arms over here – what has anyone ever done to him?"

And Neil blushed and nodded.

"I don't think he understands the people," Neil said.

"That's right – that's right," Mickey said, "He don't understand the people."

Neil had intended to say other things – had intended to get to the bottom of it all. Of course for a while he felt he had. He left for the university thinking that he had resolved matters in a comfortable, civilized way. Wind from the horse stalls blew to his nose, the chicken manure stank, and he longed never to come back again.

Another memory came to him as he drank his coffee and watched the pale snow falling, falling on the street outside.

It was a memory that encompassed everything he had been thinking about the past.

Shortly after Neil's visit home, when he had not been assaulted, Dexter had been.

At that time Neil had felt the kind of feeling he had read some place that the German word *Schadenfreude* is supposed to represent. It was the idea that he was glad a certain misfortune had happened to someone close to him rather than to himself. The feeling came that this misfortune was not visited upon him because he was somehow better than Dexter was. It was the shameful feeling people have all the time, and that he had this morning over the illness of his brother Garth.

"Yes, it's too bad, but if he had lived his life better – more proper – this wouldn't have happened to him or Vicki," he had told Anna once about Garth.

This is what he had felt at the time about Dexter. He was even so angered by Dexter's writing at that time that he had said to himself, "Well, I'll be happy when he does drink himself to death."

So Neil had put the beating down to Dexter living a dissolute life and drinking with low companions, in dark taverns and bars, and that this is what had caught up with him.

But now, this morning, he knew differently. He was glad people generally misunderstood Dexter's work. He had wanted to misunderstand it himself – only recently did he see the terrible compassion it had.

Dexter's books were always an affront to anyone who did not understand this compassion. For he wrote only about the worst side of the province.

For a long time Neil had not wanted to say anything good about these books. And then one evening, one summer evening, just last year, he read the second book, and he suddenly saw the hockey player's wife vainly, desperately, trying to act with dignity. It overwhelmed him, and tears started to his eyes. And he was embarrassed he, as a wise man, had not seen this in the work before.

He would never be able to mistake the affection Dexter had for his characters for something else, ever again.

Vicki had hated this man's work when she had first heard she had been written about, because she could not imagine herself, or anyone like her, represented as a tragic figure, and couldn't begin to read it. But again, most people who disliked him had found in Dexter a relatively soft target.

This is what Neil knew now.

Dexter had drunk all night. And at ten in the morning he was on his way home. In the small town everyone knew him but, at this time in his life, in 1980, very few spoke to him.

He had stopped to buy his mother a package of Pall Malls, which she smoked in secret. When he had come out of the store, he met two odd little characters – Penny Shackle and Louis Gatineau – standing on the sidewalk, counting up the pennies in their hands.

Dexter's heart, or sense of duty, or whatever it was, went out to them, and he rushed back into the store to buy them ice cream. He then took them to the park, where they went into the wading pool in their underwear.

Dexter was never a big man, and he was already weakened from drink. He sat on the rim of the wading pool, drinking the last of a pint of Lamb's Navy rum.

He was seen in the small park, near the wading pool, with two small children, and word began to get around.

That evening Vicki stormed into the bar, more furious than she had ever been before. The idea quite suddenly had emerged that Dexter was a pedophile. Because once something bad is believed about a certain individual, all other images of that person become incorporated into that belief.

And Mickey Dunn embraced this belief and comforted

Vicki at this moment. The idea that Vicki would need approval from Mickey Dunn was not lost on others at the bar that evening.

All the agony of Vicki's life seemed to be focused upon this wading-pool incident. Penniless, with her own husband home, also drunk, and in a fever to be someone, Vicki spoke of getting back at Dexter and getting even.

Sylvain, too, was furious, a fury born of so much injury as never to be encompassed by the world.

Vicki was still so young then, so beautiful. For many reasons she had blamed Dexter for everything. Sylvain was struck by her beauty. He wanted to perform for her, in a way to show that he was a better man than Garth Shackle.

Neither Vicki nor Sylvain nor anyone at the bar knew very much about the word pedophile. But they had all decided what Dexter was at that moment.

They waited for Dexter to come into the bar that night. And Dexter as usual arrived. As usual he was alone.

Vicki by then had thought better of it. It was said that she did try to stop them. But by then it was too late. She had started something she could not stop. And Sylvain, who was with his friend, just pushed her away.

Dexter was thrown down on the landing. He smiled to say something about Louis and Pumpkin and how he liked them, and then, half-drunk, lifted his hands to stop the blows. The Pall Malls, which he had not yet taken to his mother, fell from his pocket, as he put his hands over his head. All he could remember was Vicki screeching for him to forgive her because it was not her fault – not her fault – just like the character in his novel.

Then they unceremoniously threw him down the iron steps of the bar.


Through the 1980s, especially after Neil got tenure, Anna and Neil were happy. But Anna and Neil were also miserable. And it was this intertwining of sadness and happiness that braided their life together, as it did the lives of all married people.

Anna wore a brace and was almost blind. But their sadness came from something else entirely - something which they were immersed in, and could not extricate themselves from without hurting other people's feelings or Neil's chance for advancement.

They got into a particular group, headed by Wheem, where radical thought fell off all of them like golden coins along the hallways and meant nothing at all. Where for their certain set the whole idea of physical life was anathema.

Wheem was a most clever practitioner of this. He was also the most compassionate toward Anna now, and looked to be almost bereaved when she stumbled or bumped into something.

Sometimes when Anna was drinking she would say things about this. She disliked Wheem. She distrusted his radical thought. She mistrusted his compassion toward her. She would tell Neil that they shouldn't all be so smug just because they happened to live in houses none of them could maintain without workmen like Reggie, whom she loved, and whom none of them would spend even a second with.

She kept telling Neil that the university had other groups, other people, and that they had narrowed themselves by being part of the inner circle. That she knew people and professors outside this group twice as fine.

Anna thought the women in this group complained too much. She thought of them as women in the Mother Goose story who, trying to glitter with golden coins, got stuck with self-serving tar.

She was drinking more now. Her little body was always so tiny-looking, her small ears stuck out from her long hair. She was unhappy, and Neil knew this. Yet as Neil grew older, the world seemed to prove the Wheems out, and Wheem looked happy. His CIA novel was with Krakman's Publishing in New York, and he was showing everyone the favourable letter he had received.

During this time, a student in Neil's Canadian literature class, Tracy McCaustere, finally brought the town of Taylorville and all its problems to the university.

Tracy McCaustere was going to be a lawyer. She was going to go home to Taylorville someday and settle whatever problems had to be settled, by law, just as her father and her grandfather had done before her. She was one of the serious ones. She would look at Neil as if he had the wrong attitude about something, as if she was disappointed in him. He didn't know why this was, but he tried in certain ways to atone for something he had never done to her. And Neil knew this Holy Thursday at eight-thirty in the morning, as he stood in the kitchen drinking his second cup of coffee, patting Sebastian the cat, that at the time he had been frightened of her.

Her concern centred around a particular book. It was Dexter's third and last novel, just then published (by his third publisher). Tracy claimed it was racist because of the last four chapters. She seemed immeasurably happy because of this, and the incitement it caused.

At first no one had paid attention to her, or to the book, but after a time, Neil remembered now, she found the backing of certain people. One of these people was Christopher Wheem. She was supported a good deal by Wheem, and others, who stayed in the background.

Tracy applied to have the book removed from the local bookstore.

The owner did not remove it, but draped it in black (in order to draw attention to his store). This caused the controversy to gain wider attention. A few students threatened to boycott the owner if it wasn't removed. They gathered about Tracy, printed slogans and signs.

They wanted Neil to march with them to the store.

Neil also realized even back then that most of the people who had been against the book had not read it.

The scenes in question involved an Indian dispute over money. It involved a character very much like Reggie and a man, he supposed, quite like Peter Bathurst.

Peter Bathurst himself did not get involved when people asked him about this book.

They showed him on television shrugging and looking at his powerful hands when they asked him if he was personally upset by such a book, if there were any hard feelings.

"Oh, I don't read much," he said, and smiled. "But I might read this one."

The days were short and bitter, the snow swept inward and covered Fedder Lane where Neil and Anna still lived. Above them, upon one of the icy cliffs, a large communication tower, with a yellow light flashing in the grey afternoon, seemed to Neil to be the compelling heartbeat of men and women.

Neil fluctuated back and forth over which side to take and Anna sensed this in him. Neil realized now that she saw, could tell, and understood the countless ways in which he tried to dodge any suggestion of taking sides.

One night he went out, crossed his lane, and went up toward the beacon on the hill. He had just had an argument with Anna over the book, and he was sick at heart. Four professors had come to Dexter's defence, and he had not been one of them.

He decided that if he made it to the communication tower, to the light, he would support and teach the book – as Anna had asked him to do. If he didn't reach it, if he found he couldn't, he would not.

The sky was grey. From the back lanes, the small houses, the frozen dooryards of this Maritime community came the drizzle of foggy cold. Far away came the lonely turbulent barking of a dog.

He saw old cars up on blocks, the faces of small children in dreary windows, the eyes of men passing him – eyes quick and filled with anger.

Suddenly the road stopped, all lanes ended. Snow started to fall and it was dark. He had lost sight of the light, the communication tower. He would have to enter the woods, and climb straight up the cliff, past those broken, splintered trees he had often viewed from his living room.

He began to do this. He gave it a try. But the snow got deeper and deeper – there were no ribbons or markings to follow, only the wind grating the tops of the trees, and the forlorn yelp of a dog chained out on this bitter night.

Neil's ears began to freeze.

And suddenly he felt he could not go on into the dark, to reach the light. He turned back. Far, far below him sat Fedder Lane, with his ugly brick apartment building. It looked so small and distant.

He knew the book was not racist. He knew in fact it was probably just the opposite. He knew that Tracy McCaustere, already being groomed for law and politics, had certain motives which even she would be unsure of.

He also knew he must go to great lengths not to appear racist. He remembered a young boy Tracy egged on, with his angry blue eyes and pimpled face, standing alongside her, and he shuddered.

He turned down the lane toward home.

As he walked Neil thought back to the picture of Reggie and Timothy that he had seen on the dresser three years before. Of Reggie's innocence. That was what those scenes in Dexter's book were really about. They were about Reggie, and about his child, Diane Bartibog, whom he was never allowed to see.

But for the moment Neil pretended, like others, that truth lay somewhere else. That he was searching for truth. He did not teach or defend the book. He said nothing.

Dexter, for a number of untold reasons, was never to write another word. He went home to Taylorville a year later, and Neil never saw him again.

The next year Tracy McCaustere entered law school at Osgoode Hall in Toronto.

Now, years later, Neil remembered that he had reached that light – that communication tower – a few months later, and had felt good doing it. There was, however, by then nothing on the line.

In 1984 Neil and Anna moved into a small but comfortable brick house across the park. Neil's father, Tom, came to visit them. But while he was there he would not come out of his room at the top of the stairs, and Neil thought he must be angry with him.

"Aren't you coming down for breakfast?" Anna would ask.

"Oh, don't worry about me. I don't go about eating very much atall."

Now and then they would peek in at him, and he would

smile and wave at them from a chair. He didn't have an ashtray and butted two of his cigarettes out on a book from Neil's study. He had one of the old suitcases, and wore woollen pants and suspenders over his long underwear. All night long they could hear him coughing.

By the third day he had still not come out of his room.

Finally he told them why. He had injured himself in the barn, two weeks prior to the visit, and was in pain. But since he had promised them he was coming for a visit, he had come for a visit.

He had not urinated in three days.

"Oh, don't mind that," he said. "As long as I don't drink much I won't piss much."

They took him, in spite of his protests, to the hospital, where it was found that his kidneys were obstructed and three ribs were broken.

So old Tom's visit was mainly to the hospital.

They kept him there for two weeks, and Neil and Anna visited him there every night they could.

Tom sat amongst the other patients, smoking and talking loudly, the way he often did when he was lonely.

He talked about Garth and the great games he had seen, the trip he went on once to Montreal, how Brian Verriker the NHL star was a friend of theirs.

During the day Anna visited him, and he would introduce her to everyone. Opening up his johnnyshirt he showed her the wound on his side where he had fallen on the rake in the barn. It looked as if he had been stabbed with a pitchfork. He talked to her about bingo, and how the reserve was going to get a giant bingo hall. That this was what Peter Bathurst was up to if Diane Bartibog would help him out.

"Bingo is the thing – I shoulda got into bingo." So he talked about bingo, and Peter Bathurst running the treasury for the whole reserve, and how he himself had no problem with Peter Bathurst. That there were others, mind you – but not Peter Bathurst, no sirree.

One day when she came to visit he was staring out the window, depressed. He sighed and would not speak to her for many moments. He had turned off his hearing aid, and sat there with his eyes watering.

Then he whispered to her that he did not care to live.

He said that one time in 1961 he had struck his wife, who was trying to protect Reggie from his terrible temper. He could still feel his wife's small little hands trying to hold him back. Reggie had got an Indian girl pregnant, he told her, and Tom had had no idea what to do except to hit him. Now he knew it had been a mistake. He sighed at this.

Anna tried in her own way to tell Tom that he was forgiven, by Reggie, and his wife. But he said nothing.

"Reggie – my Reggie – has gone away," he said. He looked at her as startled as a child, and nodded, pinching a yellow smoke in his craggy fingers.


At the same time that Neil's father was there, in another corner of the large, grey, out-of-date hospital, down a corridor smelling of enclosed air and urine, Christopher Wheem sat, waiting for his child to be born. He had brought flowers, and sat in a small yellow waiting room.

A fetal monitor had been hooked up to Jenna at three in the afternoon of March 2. Now it was after eight. The contractions were still progressing, the heart of the child was strong, but something during the day had made Wheem feel frightened.

He had seen Anna walking along the corridor and had asked her to sit with him. There was no one else. His parents were nothing to him, and all of Jenna's family disliked him. He had insulted them all over the course of their marriage.

He had dressed well; his overcoat lay on the chair beside him. He was looking for a place to smoke his pipe, but now and again Jenna's moans during a contraction made him feel sick, and he looked at Anna as if wanting comfort from someone.

He had not known that pregnancy would be like this. They would have to use a needle to break her water, and had probed her with their fingers. She lay with a white sheet over her, looking about, sucking on ice, and trying to tell jokes, while she clenched her teeth in pain. She was tiny, normally 106 pounds, and was trying to be brave.

Anna stayed with her and held her hand during the contractions as Wheem stood at the door. Jenna could make out his feet beyond the blue curtain a nurse had hauled about her bed. He looked in at her and smiled timidly, and then over at Anna.

"I have to go for ice," he said.

All about was the smell of urine and of feces and the cries of newborn babies, which always sounded distant. Wheem did not like it. He tried, and Anna could tell. He tried to be there for her. He wanted to be joyous.

"I'm going to make it," Jenna whispered to Anna. "I'm not brave enough, but God will help me. You see – I'm all alone – Chris doesn't know this – but he has never been there for anyone –"

"Shhh – you are the bravest woman I know," Anna whispered, holding her hand tightly. She did not know Jenna well, yet at the moment felt close to her, and cared for her more than for anyone in the world.

Jenna had a strong French accent and once or twice burst out angrily in French, when the clumsy intern did his probe, and then burst out laughing because of the absurdity, and wonder, of her situation.

"Dere seeing all my freckles now," she kept yelling to her husband, who was standing back behind the blue curtain, with his cup of ice.

Anna went into the birthing room with her.

Their child Hector Dylan Wheem was born at 11:19 that night of March 2. They had to use forceps. The delivery table was covered with blood and feces.

The strangest thing of all was Jenna's homely red purse sitting on a corner chair.

If philosophy was air, as someone said, life, when you touched it hard, was brass.

Neil did not know this Holy Thursday when he had heard it. He was still in the kitchen, still thinking. It had come in a remote way, as things do. Like Garth's injury, long ago. Things happen and are over. Your own life becomes more important to you. You bring Pumpkin over for a visit, buy her a Louisa May Alcott book, and inscribe it, with best wishes. Something like that. The general epiphany is difficult to grasp. It is there in the hard brass air about the university buildings, the black doorways, the smell of tires from the huge tire plant, the desolate headframes of a Maritime community.

At first no one paid attention to Dexter's death. That spring afternoon when everyone was busy doing other things.

But after a time Dexter's name began to surface. Here and there. Now and again. Suddenly there was some interest in what he had said, and what he had written.

Summer came again.

It was in the middle of this summer, Neil reasoned now it was 1986, though it could have been 1987. In summer, with its listless sense of foreboding, Neil went with Anna to visit Dexter's mother. It was Anna who insisted that they go. The woman, after all, was her aunt.

They travelled home in August.

The woman sat in a chair in the den, with the window opened. She wore a blue skirt and short-sleeved white blouse. A small black wristwatch on her white bony wrist. Her hair was oval and her eyes blue.

She smiled and Neil smiled back. She had known the Shackles only by reputation. There was a slight measurement of her eye against his, a question about something unasked, and then she turned to Anna.

She said she felt she did not know much about her son, and asked Anna some questions about him.

Then suddenly she wanted to show them the room where he died.

It was a strange thing to show them, but she said many people were interested in this room. That professor Wheem had come to view it as well.

The room was bare. It overlooked the pools of placid water, the field beyond.

It overlooked the life Dexter wrote about.

The room was bare because of obstinacy and laziness and a fear of looking pretentious. There was only one small painting, of the mill stream, hanging on the wall in the far corner. An old childhood microscope sat on the desk, along with a tiny portrait of someone. The drawers had some reviews stuffed into it.

"You see," the woman said. For some reason she looked quite old suddenly. Her back was more bent than they had realized.

"This is a nice room, isn't it?" she said as she opened up the window.

She handed some of the reviews to them. Neil had forgotten or had not considered it important how slighting these reviews had been. The woman did not understand this either. Although, as she said, she thought her son might have been barking up the wrong tree.

"They want a street named after him now," she said suddenly, her eyes showing a kind of triumph at Neil's expense. "They don't know that I know they all hated him," she said.

A few years passed. For a while Neil hated the university and longed to move. Hated the town and hated the thought of going home.

For two years Christopher Wheem never spoke to him, cultivating, Neil supposed, a more important circle. Wheem lied about Neil just as he had about Dexter. For the purpose of a career seemed to be to cheat someone, anyone, it didn't matter who.

Once in a while Neil travelled away for interviews in other parts of the country, and came home. He took a sabbatical and they went to Europe for almost a year in 1987–88. They came back to the same house.

From then on the pleasure went out of life for Anna. What Neil had become was not what he had started out to be.

He, too, had not become what he had wanted to.

She quit the string quartet, and her cello sat in the closet, zipped shut in its case.

Now and then over the next year, from certain people who came and went, they would hear of the trouble on the reserve – that there was a power struggle that involved

Peter Bathurst and Diane Bartibog, people who had once been friends. That there were threats and insinuations.

"I knew that would happen – I knew it all," Neil said.

And then one morning quite suddenly they got a call from home, saying Neil's father was on his way to see them. Garth was very ill, his liver gone. It was now nine years since Neil had been home and Tom was determined to get them back.

He was taking the bus over on Holy Thursday so they would drive him home for Easter. An Easter he wanted them to spend with Vicki and Penny and Garth.

Neil woke early that morning and, after having his coffee in the kitchen, and listening to the CBC, he put on his heavy coat, and went out to the university.

Anna woke later. She was again just slightly hungover.

Outside the day looked miserable. The old Esso building, the small parking lot with its one dirty tree, and the wired streetlight at the corner, now flickering yellow, now flickering red.

She hoped they would be happy, she hoped the world would be happy again. But now it was apparent that life was not meant to be easy or happy.

Neil's life had not worked out the way he'd hoped, and he was sad.

Neil realized that the home study would take place soon, and Anna was worried about this. Because they had been wanting to adopt a child for the last five years.

Anna wore glasses so thick that people got dizzy looking through them. She had been born with a lame leg because her mother had fallen when pregnant.

More poignant was that she believed she had camouflaged her poor eyesight. She tried to camouflage her limp now, and reminded Neil to put his three diplomas on the living-room wall.

She had already gathered baby clothes and had made over a room and Neil had teased her about this.

"I don't see a baby in there yet," he would say, glancing in. "Are you sure this is the way it comes?"

She had packed to go home the night before. She felt miserable to think that Tom felt he had to come over to get them.

At midday she phoned the university. The bus would be late, for a bad storm had started up north.

However, Neil was busy, something important was happening, and he couldn't worry about the bus at the moment. There would be lots of time to go later in the day. Or perhaps on Good Friday.

Looking out the window Anna saw soft snow falling and falling. Snowflakes that in cities always smell something like gas. She had tried to make Neil happy but she could not.

For no matter what happened now, things were not the same, and she imagined would never be the same again.

She remembered the poem, by her cousin Dexter:

Fallen angels
no longer in hell with wings
in tweeds at university
complain of earth bound things.

She remembered this poem now more than ever before.

It was Holy Thursday, ten o'clock in the morning, in a town thirty miles from Taylorville and 150 miles from the university.

The snow was deep. The little buildings stretched down the street, to a cold, flat street below. The buildings were dark grey, with closed-up wooden doors. The roofs were slanted in comforting ways. Footprints led here and there and became obliterated.

Christopher Wheem, his hands in his pockets and his hat pulled down over his eyes so that only the bottom of his goatee seemed to shine in the ugly small light of the flashing restaurant sign, moved diagonally across this street and disappeared.

He was in a town on the Miramichi. Had come here to meet a woman he longed to forget. Wheem hated a town like this, for it was the kind of town he had come from, and all of his life the kind he had sought to escape. Or at least this is what he thought about the town. In actual fact, this town had nothing to do with anything he himself had known.

He crossed the street.

The wind came up and he scowled and thought of a particular song, a particular aria of an opera he had been to. Often he pretended to know a great deal about opera to himself. But when he whistled, it came out a Beatles tune.

He hugged the building's side.

For a while Wheem had tried his hand at knowing opera in order to have something more to write, more to say about the possibilities of man. But he had forgotten most of what he learned. He never thought of the opera much now. He would still go to the symphony, but it seemed not a part of him any more. Not for the last few years now.

The snow was papery soft, and fell out of the sky onto his expensive winter hat.

He had made out all right with his CIA novel for a while. Everyone was kind to him. He read a chapter on the CBC. He played the part of being famous. One thing led to another and he left his wife, Jenna, and their son, Hector. He wondered about all of this now.

The idea, of course, was twofold in his novel. The CIA was a terrible menace to Canada, which was a peace-loving country, and that was a hit with certain intellectuals who hated the States. But there was the idea as well that the CIA had meddled in Quebec's affairs, and Wheem did not know which way to go with this, and had never really resolved it. If Quebec independence was good – as certain English-Canadian intellectuals boasted, like his friend little Professor Hunt – did the CIA, which was not good, wish for it? Did the CIA wish Canada to remain united or no?

If it did want Canada united, then wasn't there still a certain grandiose idea of patriotism it was supporting?

In the end he made a compromise – the CIA got involved within both factions and kept each faction at the other's throat. This resolved any conflict Wheem had about his country while still blaming it on outside forces.

But then some years had passed. The CIA novel was forgotten. It had been remaindered. And no other novel of his had been published.

He was growing older. His wife and son had moved far, far away from the university. He was never sure where. Small lines were appearing on his face and he took pains to use cream to stay younger looking. He was, he believed, an athletic person.

He exercised well, and hardly drank. His favourite books were always new, always current. Those he loved yesterday he no longer loved today.

Each play he did with his students was always new, always current. And as with enthusiastic high-school teachers from small towns there was the sense of profound naivety in all of this. He laughed too loud, was always boasting of his connections to impressionable women, and was always vulgar. He strove not to be.

He tried to rewrite his early novel, the one he had started at university, about the aristocratic woman from

Ontario and, as this book and his course-load took its withering twists and turns, he had met Vicki Shackle.

She had come to university for one year. It was the year Anna and Neil were in Europe.

Wheem was the first professor she met. And in a way she fell in love with him.

Her husband, crippled with arthritis, after a thousand assaults upon his great body, had sold the last thing he owned – a two-year old standardbred which jogged well but raced poorly – so she could go to university. Wheem could not even conceive of this kind of sacrifice, or what it meant to her husband and child, or to herself.

She was a woman of thirty-six, who wanted suddenly to change a life she blamed on others.

She did not know that in the hands of Wheem she was to become somewhat famous.

Wheem wrote a brief but startling article on her called "When the Dream Fades." It was published in an Upper Canadian magazine. It was about the life of a woman betrayed by hockey. Later, with another article and Vicki's poems, it was published in a small chapbook.

At this time hockey was under attack from the left wing of the university and Garth's career was finished.

There were no more chances for Garth and no more friends. He worked for Mickey Dunn, and was teased by a dozen people.

Vicki knew exactly how his life had gone. The terrible-ness of it. How he had tried to make her happy. But when she went to university it seemed she forgot some of it.

Although no one at that small university was saying this, his failed career in some ways ensured a better career for Wheem and a name for herself.

She brought Wheem her poetry. It was not good poetry but that didn't matter. To Wheem it was suddenly great poetry. Other people too were saying the kindest things about her.

She wrote dozens of poems in those few months she was at university. One was entitled "Why Me." A few of them were published in that inexpensive chapbook and "Why Me" was read on the CBC. She was interviewed for the newspaper section called "Women Today." It was an exciting time for her.

Wheem had hoped she would have forgotten him by now. But the calls and letters kept coming. He longed for its end. But yesterday she phoned and insisted she see him again.

Wheem left the street he was on, and crossed to another, a smaller street with a small shopping mall, dismal because its lights were on at this time of day, dismal because the Easter Bunny carried a basket. Dismal because of everything else. And snow fell.

"It has been snowing forever in Narnia," Wheem remembered his ex-wife reading to his child. The little boy he had deserted. It was snowing forever in Narnia, and everywhere else also.

It seemed to fall into his guts as he walked. It smelled like darkness. Always there was darkness for him. He had tried to revive one novel after another – always playing catch-up with some new fashion. Always just on the outside, always trying new things. Nothing seemed to work for him now. His agent in New York was gone. His last novel unfinished.

He sometimes thought of his little boy, and how he looked, with his mother, waiting for the train to come.

There was hardly a train in Canada any more – the trains had all but stopped, but she had wanted to take the train for some reason Wheem wasn't sure about. Of course it was to spite him in some way, Wheem thought.

She was an Acadian girl from the northern region of the province, and Wheem had given himself certain airs when he married her. They'd had a large wedding – a fine reception. Like everything else Wheem did there was something vulgarly fashion-conscious in it.

But he had married the wrong girl. Jenna had a piety that he could not understand, nor did he want to. The idea that she would be good for his career down here in the Maritimes was not as true as he had hoped. He had secretly hoped that marrying an Acadian girl was the right thing to do.

And then when the child was born with Down's syndrome, it was a terrible blow. He could stand much, but not that.

There was anger on his face whenever he thought of it. He, of course, had tried to sue the doctors and the hospital.

The litigation went on and on and on, and petered out, but for months on end he couldn't look at the child without feeling betrayed. It was not that he did not care for the boy. No one could say he did not care for him. Yet he could not (and he believed he tried to) understand the love Jenna had for him.

And so the boy and his mother went. They went on the train in the evening almost six years ago. It was snowing that night as well.

So he became free to pursue other things. And the years passed along. The divorce became final.

The heart-wrenching story had circulated through the department that his wife, knowing the child's condition from the third month, refused to "do the right thing," and that Wheem, in his fine clothes, his tailored three-piece suit, had agonized with her over this for months, but could not convince her of a proper course of action. And suddenly Wheem was viewed as both moral and compassionate because of this.

But then at the train station. That was the most terrible thing. Waiting with them there, and all of those people. People she felt comfortable with, no doubt, but people he did not associate with himself. She broke into French with one balding young fellow in a Ski-doo suit and he laughed gaily and offered the boy candy.

The boy with those awful tubes in his red ears timidly smiling up at his father. And worse, Wheem's affected unnatural smile as the balding man in the Ski-doo suit picked the boy up and genuinely hugged him.

It was snowing forever in Narnia because something had taken hold of Wheem, and things were dying slow.

Vicki was supposedly waiting for him at the small motel at the end of a snowswept back street. He had not seen her in six years or so. His life had gone along, become more important to him, but she could not see it. He was afraid of her in a way. But the real truth was he thought she was vulgar and misunderstood his finer feelings, and now he was afraid she would embarrass him.

He'd met Garth once. To Wheem, Garth did not look like a "real" human being. His hands had been battered and his nose flattened to one side. He had drifted down and down so that even the Roanoke Rebels of the Southern Hockey League – a farm team of a farm team – no longer required his services. And there he was in the middle of winter, sitting in a small chair, with Vicki looking disheartened that he had come to visit her while she was at university studying humanities.

Wheem was to take her to a poetry reading that night in 1988 and he entered the apartment with a smile. He had been wearing his cape, which he wore at that time to poetry readings. Since most poets were better than he was, he wanted to show his eccentricity, and the first thing Wheem had seen was a young girl who looked up incredulously at him. A girl with big brown eyes.

Because Garth was there, she and Wheem didn't know what to do or say to each other. Garth even seemed to be embarrassed that he wanted a moment with Vicki alone;

that he and their daughter had come over for a visit. He looked lonely, and a pack of playing cards was stuck in his shirt pocket. He did not mention hockey. Though there was a game on the television it seemed he didn't even notice it.

Besides Wheem had become a baseball fanatic and followed the Milwaukee Brewers. He always mentioned his achievements in baseball terms; i.e., that he was batting very well.

Vicki for her part found that by mentioning her child's name in a certain way, she could gain sympathy. Children as burden, and as pain, had become part of her curriculum vitae.

Wheem lit a small pipe and hurried on now.

It didn't seem like it would end snowing. And by evening, they said, the storm would reach south. That meant that the road would be hard to pass, and it might be blocked.

He hated it here. What this town proved was that at any given second the country could become isolated and unlivable. And you and your family and a variety of plants and animals could freeze to death in a second.

Wheem fidgeted in his heavy coat and expensive hat. He hadn't thought of it as Holy Thursday until this moment, when he turned and saw the motel in the distance. It looked vaguely surreal, hidden as it was up a side street between the drifts, snow blowing like smoke from their tops.

Vicki had driven thirty miles, from Taylorville, to meet

him. He had written the name of the motel, "The Waverley," on his notepad. She sounded desperate to meet him but he had not wanted to be seen with her at the university – he was engaged to one of his students now, and he was a little worried that Vicki might arrive at some inconvenient time.

He wanted only one thing: to find rest from Vicki before something embarrassing happened, and to leave and never come back. She had written him thirty-seven unanswered letters in the last five years. *All my love, Vicki. Yours completely and forever, Vicki. Guess who?*

What would he deny? The affair? Well, of course now he couldn't. But he would finally have to deny something else, and that was his commitment of love that he had once said he had for her. Both had pretended to have been hurt in the same way, by the same things. So she wrote poems, and he another novel, and they pretended. They lived a dissolute delusion, north of anywhere that seemed to matter in the kind of world where he really wished to belong. But essentially it was what he and everyone he knew had done all of their lives. From the time of his protests against the Vietnam war on.

He had no idea about this town but he had some idea that his ex-wife lived in a town quite similar to this, somewhere to the north.

Only he could not get over the look of sorrow on his son's face at the train station. It bothered him now, and it bothered him every day. He tapped his pipe against a store's black wall. The snow shone white where the coals fell.

He owned a large house near the university, and three more besides, that he rented to students – female students. This was where he had met his fiancée. He liked the long avenues of the university town. He considered himself a socialist. He was always the first to speak up about someone's rights.

He'd been in business with Ubo Gail, the economics professor, who always spent lavish amounts of money. Wheem had always defended Ubo Gail until recently. Recently the bank took over the properties, and Wheem realized he was out some thirty-two thousand dollars.

People did not know how closely Wheem monitored his small business affairs. He was in fact very tight with his money, something his fiancée was becoming aware of. This loss of money was an awful thing. The bank had sent a detective to talk to him, who told him Ubo Gail was wanted for questioning.

He had already tried to write about it, but he was too sick at heart and too ashamed of his actual feelings of superiority over Mr. Gail.

He thought again, as if to ease some terrible feeling inside, of his son, Hector. He remembered the day his wife had been trying to teach the boy his numbers. He was sitting at the table with a crayon. His hair was sandy blond. His eyes were small, his nose blunt. He waddled like a duckling when he walked and was forever smiling.

Hector was smiling, holding the page in his hand, when his father came through the door. It had been a bad day. Wheem had lost an argument with one of his students over Dexter. And more than anything he wanted to impress his students.

Wheem did not realize how livid this had made him, and he took it out on his son. He tore the paper from his boy's hand and threw it on the floor, and, smashing his fist down on the table, shouted: "Stop! NO MORE!"

And as always, anger captivates those who are angry.

The child looked at his paper with the numbers on them, and looked at his mother.

His mother had practised with him and he had managed to make two numbers – the 1 and the 5 – the 5 upside down. It was not an unusual mistake, but to Wheem it became symbolic of their misfortune.

It was over. Wheem's lips trembled above his goatee as he tried to smile and he apologized. He really did apologize, but to no avail; the boy was frightened of him.

Lately he'd been remembering the incident more and more, and strangely he had been missing his son more as well.

He had recently told of this incident to a friend who had come to the university on a reading tour. His friend had a new book out that had been reviewed well in the *New York Times*. Wheem had told the man about this incident with his son, as if confessing some betrayal from his past, only to have the young man smile slightly.

And Wheem realized how tragic his life was at this moment.

He pressed on, the wind under his large coat.

It was snowing forever in Narnia. Because, although he

was trying not to, he was falling away from something else, and something which he'd always thought he would be included in. And that was the inner circle at the university. He did not know why. Perhaps someone had mentioned something. But one night at the restaurant, Le Chateau, he had an inclination that he had failed in some dramatic way. He saw a certain look of mild-mannered recrimination on certain faces toward him, that he had once exhibited toward others.

Wheem began to feel that something would show him up. He was beginning to see that the university might fail the Wheems of the world, as well as the Dexters. He tried to go over his cards, wondering, at night alone, which ones it was that he hadn't played quite right.

Almost no one in this cluster of small river towns, with their paper mills and shopping malls, would have any idea of what Wheem did.

That he spent a good deal of his time going to conferences to give papers on writers. When he did he travelled on government money. His salary was large and for life. Although many at the mill would earn as much, a mill could shut down. Wheem's world didn't face shutdown.

Nor, more often than not, did it have anything to do with the life it was pretending to examine.

Wheem knew about writers no one knew, and films no one saw.

Wheem had reached middle age, and what a frightening place it was.

Vicki had seen in him not a Hun, but something of a Roman citizen. His soft hands and his beard that covered up the downy cheeks like a middle-aged woman's, his diffident, not unfriendly eyes.

She had come from a world so unfamiliar to him that he might have turned pale. For her husband to be knocked in the head, to have his ankle rebroken, and play upon it, to throw up blood an hour before he went onto the ice – that was her world. It was not Wheem's.

And Vicki longed for a gentle world. The world outside. The thing was, her husband had continued for years to try to give this world to her, though he was ill and ashamed.

Wheem turned where the snow had settled over a footpath and crossed the frozen road. To his left the huge river sat as mysterious and as cold as stone. To his right all the small buildings and stores he had passed lay settled down and coddled by the snow.

Vicki was sitting on one of two chairs with her back to the closed curtain, her cigarette going in the ashtray. There was a picture of a seagull in flight on the wall above her head.

"I'm sorry I couldn't a metcha in a better place – ya probably think some bad a me," she said. He had forgotten her heavy accent that cut across the grain of her beauty.

The small room, with the desperate orange bedspread, was filled with cigarette smoke, and she lit another cigarette.

Wheem waved his hand and took off his fur-lined

gloves. He had a look, as always, of moderate surprise and desperation on his face. He sat down on the edge of the bed and looked behind him quickly, then looked at her a moment. He reached for something in his pocket that was bothering him, and shifted it over. He sighed as if he was very upset. Vicki noticed this and tried to smooth her hair. She looked here and there. In the grey light she looked old now, especially around her mouth. And Wheem had always been attracted to younger women; his fiancée was twenty-six.

"Did you get my poem?" she asked.

"No, I didn't," Wheem said. Then to keep up the pretence of encouragement he added, "So you're writing poems again – that's great." She told him she had brought all of her poems with her. They were in a box in the car.

She looked at him with hauntingly sad eyes, and he looked away.

Of course, they were supposed to get married – run away together, all of that. Wheem did not know she would have taken all of that seriously (or he had convinced himself he didn't know) until her letters started. Now quite suddenly he blurted out that he was engaged.

"A wonderful woman," he heard himself saying, "someone to straighten me around –" He heard himself laughing. He felt his eyes shifting. "It's troubled me at times how you and I drifted apart – but things can't be changed now," he added.

He didn't say that he had come here because he was frightened about the urgency he sensed in her letters, and worried that she might do something erratic that would hamper his plans. Like kill herself. That sounded too chauvinistic perhaps. *Don't go and kill yourself.*

He smiled again at how his plans were going, and looked about the room, as if to say *Any decent person would not want to ruin my plans.*

She was wearing tight jeans and mukluks. She had taken the mukluks off and had placed them in the corner of the cheerless room. She was the only woman he had ever known to wear mukluks. Her coat was opened and she sat with her legs slightly apart. She once had a larger-than-average diamond on her hand, and Wheem had always been intrigued by it – but this diamond ring was not there.

He did not like her now. All that had once attracted him to her had vanished, and he looked upon her now as an animal. He couldn't help this, either.

"What's in the poem?" he said, smiling slightly.

"Oh, it's about us – and how we bent the rules," she said. "It's called 'Bending the Rules.' I'm sorry but it rhymes." She smiled.

There was a long pause.

"I wasn't mentioned?" he said looking at his feet.

"Oh, no no no – but you see – it's about us."

He was worried about his impending marriage. He had to meet his future in-laws the next day. His young fiancée was spoiled and wanted things for herself. Already there had been one terrible scene in a restaurant over chocolate cheesecake.

Of course, Vicki's child must be grown up now – not so much younger than his fiancée. He thought of asking about Pumpkin and then did not. He had heard of the terrible beatings Pumpkin took at her mother's hands, and now when he looked at Vicki, at her hands, at her short flat hair, it all seemed true.

"That's what I wanted to say – about university, you know – how we went about bendin the rules." She lit a cigarette off the butt of the one before.

"Oh, university. University is terrible. I can't wait to be done with it," he said. And he proceeded to tell her that he was working on a new novel, that he now had connections, and that he soon would be out of the university and gone from the Maritimes.

He had told her most of this before, and they fell back into the comfortable lies for a second.

He knew that she wanted to ask him something. He didn't know what. And then, just as she was about to speak, he spoke.

His speech now was that something grave and wonderful had happened between them, which, because of circumstances, had not worked out. That it was not meant to be, not because of their lack of commitment, but because of other unseen things, and events. But that they would still be friends, and great friends – and she had his undying respect, forever.

There was a long pause, an all-encompassing silence as he sat there, with that cumbersome envelope in his coat pocket.

"Thanks for writing the story in the magazine about me," she said, standing. "I'll always remember that – and the chapbook, no matter what."

He didn't kiss her. He thought he might. But she turned suddenly and hugged him – almost in terror. And then, suddenly, he was alone.

The wind came more severely against him after he left. It blew through his coat and the bits of snow were raw.

Wheem was happy that he was away from her and out of it. Without too much trouble. He suspected that it was because he told her of the engagement.

Wheem did not know that she had loved him so much, until now, or loved some idea of his gracious learning, his doctorate degree.

At one point she had mentioned her husband having the indentation of a puck on his face, and Wheem had tried to suppress a smile. Now he was conscious of how his friend had suppressed the smile when he had spoken almost in tears about his son, and the tubes sticking out of his son's little red ears.

He turned and went to the bus station.

It was almost empty. The hard plastic seats in a long row. The wicket was closed. A few packages sat against the wall. Two old men sat there – a small man, with a hard-looking face, and an Indian man in a beaver hat – who seemed to know each other.

On occasion Wheem tried to find moral comfort in his reading. He tried to understand why his boy was retarded, and why this had caused the breakup of his marriage. He wanted to find out why his schemes never seemed to work out in the end. And in his readings there was one answer, which he tried to dismiss or distort.

God did not create men to be comfortable but to be great.

He had run away from this idea when he had left his child at the train station that night.

Now it was almost one in the afternoon. He learned that the bus would be delayed. And once it got here they would have to take another route. The storm, as in Narnia, was everywhere. He stood outside the bus station with nowhere to go. The sky was heavy, like when he was a child. When he was a child they used to sit in the front room and look out the window at the traffic becoming snarled.

He started walking, with his scarf pulled up over his ears, and holding onto his hat. (He looked like he wished to nod to someone but didn't quite know it.) And the wind blew his coat, and buffetted him here and there.

He did not know much about Garth but he'd been told they received money from strangers who'd remembered him in the famous game against the Russians – for some things are not forgotten. But then they had got into heroic trouble with debts. Wheem thought those must all have been eased or erased by now.

Then Wheem tried to think of pleasant things. But most of his thoughts had to do with his son.

His wife was in labour for fourteen hours. All that pain

and blood and suffering for a child she held dearer than a Mozart. Wheem put on his gloves, which still were stiffly new.

Wheem had often dreamed of having a child who was a Mozart. It was three minutes after the birth that they realized there was something terribly wrong with this one.

Wheem then thought his friends would all laugh at him. He would listen to the doctors, sitting in offices in Halifax and Toronto. He held a pained expression on his face, trying to look nurturing and helpful, but not knowing how, which made it all abysmally comic.

When they took the child to Toronto, he had a friend at the university they stayed with. Wheem as always tried to affect graciousness and propriety – tried to prove that though he lived down in the boonies, he was still quite a man. But his friend had become an academic success, while Wheem was perceived as floundering in a career in the Maritimes. He had spoken out against people in the Maritimes to prove himself to his friend, who had a puffy, arrogant face. And they both laughed.

Jenna was ashamed of him for ignoring the boy. Every day she sat in the Toronto Hospital for Sick Children alone. Wheem went about town and spoke about his CIA novel instead.

It was about to be published at that time. And as always there was an almost insane rapacious ego about Wheem whenever anything of his was about to be published. This was countered, however, by a longing to be loved for what he did.

The idea of Wheem's work was much like the idea of the unfunny comic, who is funny because he is unfunny.

Some of the sexually explicit passages in the book were so sexless he had burst out laughing at them himself. Unfortunately, like the comic who gets laughs because he isn't laughed at, Wheem did not know the scenes were bad until it was pointed out to him.

And in the end he went home, ill-tempered with both his wife and son, and blaming them for his failure.

It was a few years later that Vicki first said hello to him.


Because of his disappointment, all of his and Vicki's self-ishness seemed moral to him. Not only moral, but proper – the absolute thing to do.

At the university – the place where he had staked his whole life – his amorality had become moral; and he had treasured this intellectual comfort.

All of a sudden people were saying how moral, how comforting he was to women and he, in his three-piece suit, began to believe this also. It didn't matter if it was true. Only that it didn't have to be true if people believed it.

For a while Vicki, because of her husband's broken bones, looked much like Wheem did because of his son's disability. Both were seen as persecuted, without bearing the pain.

But how soon did it become what it was? She clung to him, not because of love, but because of a certain sense that he continually owed her an explanation for what had happened between them.

The thing was, the viciousness of it all in the end.

"I'd have a real child for you," Vicki told him once. "If you want."

As was said, Wheem had tried to find comfort in his reading. And this was hard for him because, in reality, he had long ago given up reading. And even when he did read he only liked to take out of such reading as what made him feel good.

At first he had thought: "Be not deceived – God is not mocked/ Whatever a man soweth, he shall also reap" had meant his retarded child. (He had come across this line in a hotel-room Bible one night.) But now he realized something more. Far from what he initially thought, his child might be a blessing. No, it was about him and Vicki those lines were written. Not because of what they had done together, not because of the sex, but because of what they had failed to do for those who had loved them.

Still, at this moment, something was bothering him; it was as if he was in a mystery that involved a life-and-death struggle and he was just becoming aware of it.

He had read a line last week from a fragment of Euripides, and over and over again he whispered it through his thin white lips as he walked; hardly knowing he was saying it, only aware his lips were moving:

If heaven care not for me and my two boys
There must be some good reason even for this.

Today Vicki had not made a scene as he had expected she would. But he wondered why he had dismissed so much of what she had said as not pertaining to him, when now, a short time later, it was all becoming clear. She was, and she had been, speaking to him all along, begging him for help.

"I'm glad you wrote that article on me – no matter what."

What did that mean but that her life had been altered and perhaps destroyed by the article? An article that had become so fashionable it was still being reprinted. And that articles such as it had always destroyed lives, or tried to, and in fact no one had written an article such as it for truth alone. In fact he had tried his best to slant the article to make her husband look ridiculous, and to paint him in the worst light.

He shivered as he walked.

She had smiled too today, after certain phrases she spoke, staring straight at him in a sudden desperate way – as if to make him understand, without asking him for a favour.

"Garth and I is up against her now," she had said, in her heavy accent. Why hadn't he realized she was asking him for something?

He had claimed to know all about her terrible life and wrote about it for magazines. But he couldn't even begin to write her dialogue.

He started back toward the motel, but then decided that since she had gone it would be too late to offer help.

He turned, put his cold pipe in his mouth, and wondered what to do. It looked as if there was a giant abyss between one set of snowdrifts and another; and he decided not to cross the street.

He had nothing to do but go back to the bus depot and sit down.

He went back to the depot and looked about hopefully for a sign of the bus driver. The two old men he had seen earlier stared at him.

Wheem pretended not to see them, and brushed the snow from his pants. He was nervous for some reason. Men like these had always made him nervous.

He was also aware just briefly – after he had composed himself – that this was much like a scene in Dexter's first novel, *The Bald Hills*, which ended with a bus drive. A novel Wheem had secretly tried to manipulate public opinion against. (He'd had his academic friend write a devastating review of it. It was something he didn't think Dexter ever knew.) But now this didn't seem to matter. Dexter was no longer here to fight back or to care. The day was going on.

Men – the kind of men Wheem disliked and feared – would now be responsible for getting him home. And all of this Dexter had written fifteen years before.

Wheem sat down with his legs crossed at his ankles, staring at his rubbers.

The old white man looked like an elf, albeit a tough one, with his hat on sideways and his jeans covered in snow. He smelled, even from this distance, and in the cool white bus depot, of horsehide, and dark endless barns that Wheem had sometimes passed as a boy.

The Indian man, sitting three seats further down, sometimes spoke to the old white man while the old white man would nod and speak back. Whenever this happened Wheem would look over and smile. But he was uncomfortable with men like this and could never speak to them.

Yet Vicki had known men like this all of her life. He reflected briefly on this and was glad to be gone from her.

Excepting Wheem was a card-carrying member of the NDP, the socialist party of Canada, and so he believed in an intellectual way that he knew what these men's needs were.

They were talking about the bus now. Even the graders would pull off the road now, the Indian man said, passing his old acquaintance a cigarette out of a freshly opened package.

The lines would be down too, the old man said. What chance would the bus have to get through?

Wheem did not know who to get angry with. What a foolish thing he had done in coming here. The primitive plastic seats annoyed him, the lights, the boxes piled up in front of the wicket door – and worst of all the unconcerned look on the face of the attendant inside, going about his business and getting ready to have his lunch.

"Why can't someone be concerned about me?" Wheem thought.

Though maybe his son had cared for him. That little child with the hunched shoulders and huge smile.

Hector had wanted a puppy but Wheem wouldn't hear of it: "I'm having no goddamndable puppy in my residence," he'd said, stamping his foot for show.

He took off his apricot scarf and folded it and opened his lined coat, and looked over his shoulder quickly. The man, the sour-looking little elf, smiled at him again, and went on talking about horses to the Indian man.

A great howling wind came up, and battered the windows. The wind reminded him of a night at Le Chateau.

Since outside life was so unbecoming to them they inhabited another life – an inner circle of lives grouped together. There were those who wrote passionately about the injustice of all things, without ever leaving their office.

Wheem was one of those people.

One night they were at Le Chateau. Wheem was a force there, someone to be reckoned with.

At Le Chateau he could tell a joke and everyone – the young women especially – would sit up and listen. And he never missed a night. And of course he always had a column in the *Bugle*.

One night when they were there to hear his new poems, a wind came up and a storm wrapped the outside. The lights went out, and Wheem got a candle from the kitchen and everyone gathered about it. Wheem's shadow with its stork-like appearance seemed to hover like an apparition over everything. It was one of his happiest moments. He was at the centre of things, telling impressionable young kids what to do, to start a poetry reading in the dark.

Suddenly several men came in and told them they could not leave the restaurant until they got the power lines back up. One of these chaps (as Wheem called him) was no more than eighteen.

Someone suggested they all watch the men from a window, and open another bottle of wine. And this they did.

The wine was opened. The young man of eighteen climbed up into the darkness, the storm raging, into the face of the wind, and all the trees grating around him, to unhook a line, far above the earth.

Everyone had forgotten Wheem. It was his night, but no one was thinking of him, so fascinated were they by the men outside. Wheem poured more wine, smoothed his goatee, and lifted the glass to let the candlelight splinter through it. Suddenly he began to tell an anecdote about himself, to himself.

The boy brought the line off all right and a chainsaw started. In the howling wind the boy stood atop a branch at least eighty feet above the street, and they could hear him singing in the storm.

It was at this time that things at home were bad for Wheem. He was tortured. He wanted to flee, run to Toronto. But here he was stuck in the Maritimes with a pious wife and a retarded son.

It was just after that night at Le Chateau that he began

to refuse to eat with them. The little boy would stare at his father's empty seat at the table.

Wheem went out and bought his own groceries and used half the fridge for himself. (He bought a good deal of exotic food.)

He blamed her for Toronto. He blamed her that his academic friend was editing a series of articles to be published in New York. He was alone.

And then he and Vicki became each other's victims.

For a time the beauty of her body startled him. But then he read the terrible poem.

It had been written on the stall of one of the men's washrooms and he had seen it there one afternoon, just as he was finishing his business.

> WHEEM – the kind of man
> Certain students wish to become
> Conceit without cocaine
> Vulgarity without the rum
>
> On the darkest winter street
> All of us in hat and boots
> Wheem rides his bike to class
> Tightassed in his three-piece suit.

He did not know who wrote the poem and he could not find out. Secretly he blamed a hundred people. He could not go into the common room without suspecting everyone in there. For a while he began to mark his students and judge them more harshly. He felt betrayed by his bicycle and by his life.

He saw in every student's writing the trademark of the poet. At night he would go home to a house that was almost always in darkness. His wife would look at him in smiling grief and go out to seven-o'clock mass.

His little boy with tubes in his ears – they kept draining things away from him – would look up, and quickly look at the floor, as if he knew in his heart that his father was ashamed of the tubes, but there was nothing he himself could do.

This state of affairs lasted nine months.

He slept at the far end of the house. He had his own entrance. He came and went. He was bothered by his failure.

His agent said he had done his CIA novel just a year too late (or so it seemed). And then the baseball novel too.

He ate alone at Le Chateau, and had the bad habit of nibbling his soup. He was going bald.

And then everything became resolved. Wheem had never made any distinction between religions. But now it seemed quite evident that his plans and hopes had been thwarted because she was Catholic. How had he not seen this before?

Anti-Catholicism was bubbling up amongst the intellectual class and suddenly he was swept into taking advantage of it.

He came and went from the university halls, bearing his cross. No one mentioned his son, but Wheem had the tired look of a patient man driven beyond patience. People reiterated the sentiment that he was kind and saintly.

It was, and strangely it was, because of his son, who could not yet walk very well, the greatest moral victory in his life. He found he had to say nothing, and pretended he had nothing to say.

One night his wife was sitting in the living room when he came home. She had made him dinner, she said. She said she had hired a babysitter – and if he wanted to go to that movie, the new one everyone was talking about?

It was the first time she had approached him in months. As she spoke he looked at her. She looked humble and kindly, and he felt sad he had caused her pain. But for some reason he couldn't show this.

"Sorry, I don't believe in your resurrection," he said, and he pointed to the boy. It was almost the same tone of voice he had used with Neil Shackle in his room so long ago, and he realized this and his mouth twitched. Then, still playing a part he didn't understand, he left the house again. There was a fascination with himself, a terrible glee.

He walked about in the cold air for a while. He smelled snow far off in the night and the wind started.

When he came back, she was packing to leave. A huge trunk had been pulled from upstairs. He remembered when he had put that trunk away, and how she had held his feet when he was on the stepladder. She had packed only a dishtowel.

At the university the rumour spread that a terrible fight had ensued over her religion, and she had been unreasonable. Wheem, when he was next seen, looked broken-hearted.

Often, after all the furor had died down, he was.

He had tried to find his boy a dozen times, but to no avail. And now he was sorry. But there was nothing he could do. It was over and he had done what he had done.

"I have not sinned a great deal," Wheem once wrote. "I just have not recognized things – if I had recognized that trouble would come to others because of my life, I would have acted better. I am very angry that things have not turned out for ME, you see. I would like to sleep in peace just one night without thinking of you. I don't know the nature of sin. I have tried to – but I have existed in a public way amongst other people – a practical and utilitarian way, I suppose. It was, for a long while, good enough.

"Forgive me for this as I make my way through the snow, to Le Chateau."

This was the letter in the envelope that had bothered him in his overcoat pocket.

He had written this unmailed letter to his son because in his son's face he had seen the only unconditional love ever offered to him – Wheem, the writer – by anyone. And in turn these were the only true lines he had ever written.

Vicki was now a hanger-on at the only bar in Taylorville. She had fallen through the grate into the drab world she had known as a youth. She was a gold-digger, except, for the last six years, she had been digging gold to give back to Garth.

"I'll just get the money and pay back everything all at once," she had thought a dozen times.

Vicki pulled the car to the side of the road, butted her cigarette, and smoothed her short-cropped black hair. She reached into her pocket and found her Insta-pic lotto ticket, and, taking a coin, scratched at it furiously. As long as she was scratching there was the hope of a hundred thousand dollars. She tossed the ticket aside.

She then looked for another cigarette and touched a knife in her purse. She had carried that little knife since she had been threatened by one of the men at the bar. She thought that the knife would make her safe. She looked in the mirror.

"I'm going to university, too," she had told Anna, in

excitement, in the summer of 1987, just before Anna left for Europe with Neil. "I'll show you guys a thing or two."

She had liked to pretend that Wheem would meet her at Le Chateau. But actually he never met her there, she simply arrived when he was there. He would sit with his soup in front of him. How wonderful it was for her to be in such a place. Sometimes they would all drink creme de menthe. And she liked its taste on her tongue.

She rented a small room at the edge of town. She bought a bottle of creme de menthe and kept it on her dresser. The room overlooked what she had known all of her life – a field of pit-props. She lived in a small room, with a bed and a chest of drawers, a picture of Pumpkin.

Garth had taken one of the fine colts and sold it so she could come to study. That he had to go back to sweep up at Mickey Dunn's she was to realize later. That is, that he swept up for her.

She had arrived at the university early, and the streets were bare of the congested traffic they would have a week later. Neil and Anna were in Europe, so she would not get to see them.

She had three suitcases and a handbag in her room. And she had put two of the suitcases under her cot. But no matter what she did you could tell that they were there.

She always pretended Wheem met her at Le Chateau, but she realized now that this was not really true. When she saw him earlier today in the motel, she did not know what she had *ever* been attracted to. This was why she had looked at him in terror. Nor did she tell him that his ex-wife, Jenna, and retarded son lived on the Greb Road, a mile and a half from Taylorville.

At university the earth had smelled damp and sweet. And every second building seemed to house crafts – as if this was the town of crafts people. She bought perfumed soap and a small handmade leather change purse. All the craft shops had knick-knacks and bells over the door, silent dolls with wooden eyes, and long matches, candle-holders, and something or other from Kenya.

She had walked up to look at the new university building, indolent in the sunshine, the many walkways, the small ivy-covered library.

There was an old janitor inside the door of the main building, and it was a strange mistake that became their secret. She thought he was a professor, and began to show him her ID – freshly printed – and ask him questions. One night, he acknowledged her when she was with Professor Wheem and she turned her head busily. Though she had tried to make it up to him later, it was never ever the same.

It is hard to recover from a belittlement to the spirit of kindliness.

She fell in love with Garth at fourteen, would go to the rink and freeze her feet watching him skate backwards, as his brother Reggie flipped pucks his way. He would catch the pucks on his stick effortlessly and toss them against a net made out of potato sacks and twine. It was amazing to watch him. He looked so free. He seemed to devour the ice, the wind in his eyes.

And she always wanted to be free. In fact that's why she married him. To be free, of her father and his small butcher shop, of her mother and her small envy. Of the little house with its couch covered with plastic and its constant smell of wind and vinegar.

At thirty-six she fell in love with the crafts displayed at Le Chateau. She longed to go there – especially when she heard they had literary gatherings on Tuesday nights.

The essential idea was that she had an opportunity to start her life completely over.

She peeked in the window of Le Chateau a few times but didn't dare go in. It was a cosy, small, pretentious Maritime university restaurant that like most of them was close to the street. You walked by it, and there it was.

The place was filled with talk and gentle laughter. It was filled also with slightly American, British, and Welsh accents.

"This must be the top two per cent," she thought. Her mother had always told her she must strive to be in the top two per cent. Yet the top two per cent didn't seem to be from here. They seemed to be, as always, from somewhere else.

One day she heard about a professor, Christopher Wheem, who was a fine writer. Because she had always written poems, she wanted to meet him.

"He wrote a novel on the CIA," she had been told.

Sometimes he walked by her in his three-piece suit, smoking his pipe. The aroma of tobacco filled the fall air, and the leaves sounded crisp under his feet.

The crafts in the windows displayed in their futility not only the hands that moulded them but the spiritual dearth and vanity of the age.

At Le Chateau most of the British professors thought of hockey the way most people think of boxing. Their idea also was that European hockey was much more civilized; for instance, that the Europeans had taught us grace and finesse in the age of Lafleur and Orr.

Baseball was the sport for intellectual men, and, for a certain set, cricket.

"What exactly is it you ice-hockey wives do?" a British professor asked her.

Vicki tried to explain, became flustered, looked about and saw a piece of sky-blue pottery on the window sill. At that moment she felt stifled, and alone.

"Hockey wives –" she began.

"Good God, woman, don't explain it all to me. I don't wish to know."

And there was great amusement over this remark. At Le Chateau things were like this.

At Le Chateau she told her story to people to get back at Garth. It wasn't the story she started out to tell – it was really the story her new acquaintances preferred to hear. And after a time, Professor Wheem became interested in this story. She did not know then that it was for his own advantage these questions were asked. That the idea was to do a little hockey book, to counter the one done by Dexter.

"Hockey Life a Sham," read an article in the Moncton

paper, while the Halifax papers all carried his story, and his longer article, "When the Dream Fades."

From home there was silence.

During Tuesdays and Thursdays, when Wheem wasn't overburdened by university affairs, they went for walks in the park.

In October the wind was cold, but the sun still shone warm against their backs.

The sun came through the trees and darkness lingered in the frosty branches. By the pond there was a park bench hidden under a bridge.

Wheem would often bring a bottle of coffee liqueur. And she would sometimes drink it all. She loved to drink, and could outdrink Wheem easily. Once, however, she got very drunk, and he was embarrassed by this because she roared and sang.

However, they both suffered together, she and Wheem, and it was wonderful. Yet when the articles and letters started to come back from friends of Garth who were in the NHL, from players and their wives who knew her, when she was ridiculed as a hanger-on, a gold-digger who had betrayed her husband – Wheem was not there any more. Only Garth remained.

Poor Wheem – he just ran away.

And so she was trying to forget it. She had forgotten much of it already.

For instance she had forgotten that Pumpkin had visited her four times. She had remembered only once.

Vicki had fallen down a dark grate, beating her wings against the iron bars looking for the gold that wasn't there.

The tavern was coppertone in the storm, with its signs of hunting and fishing and letters of congratulation from certain well-known locals to the owner. The stiff chairs were all placed against the tables at this early hour, and there was the ever-present smell of stale beer and pickled eggs, and the hum of a machine somewhere in the back.

Vicki entered the bar with all the majesty she could muster. She had never had any idea that all her life she walked with this majesty. Nor had she any idea that things would come to this crisis. That, because she had signed that silly "once in a lifetime" contract, she would have to pay the money this soon. She did not think she would have to invest anything in their stupid casino until after the stupid casino was built and she began to reap a benefit from it. What she had thought was that they would come over to her house after the casino opened, give her a cheque for so much, and say: "Oh, by the way, we took the twenty thousand out."

It was a very terrifying thing, now that the casino wasn't going to be built. She had heard this three weeks ago, and had hardly slept since. She had sneaked about for a day or two, trying to play the punch boards and the video machines.

But when she went for a beer one day, Mickey Dunn simply said: "Well, we all paid – we all lost – it's your turn." And he laughed as if it was a big hoot.

"Your turn" sounded like a game she played in the barn as a child where she would close her eyes and they would spin her around until she got dizzy.

But all she had managed to do was puke. That was unladylike, she knew.

She walked now with a kind of feminine impunity into a bar she had once thought she owned. She walked slowly, purse at her side. The bar was nothing like Le Chateau.

Peter Bathurst watched her enter, with small, black, deft eyes. Earlier, he had taken his father, Bruce Walk on a Cloud, to the bus station, in the rare hope he would be able to find money down south. Peter had got stuck on the way back and needed the help of a truck to get him onto the road again. His boots were covered in snow, his hair was wet, his arms folded.

Even if Vicki had a few thousand it might satisfy them. This was what Peter was thinking now. Peter himself did not have a cent. *Just a few thousand – even five thousand,* he thought.

"Hello," Mickey Dunn said, not looking at her, and doing something else. He was very short and heavy-set, had a babylike complexion and darting, almost mechanical-looking eyes, as if he was worried they would light on something too long and give him away. Vicki sat down and glanced at Peter. Her bottom lip trembled just slightly, before she broke into a smile, like the smile of a synchronized swimmer.

"I got it," she said.

"You got it," Peter said.

"Of course I got it – I can have it by Monday. I told you I would get it – so I see no reason to bother Garth or anyone else. Can I have a match – who has a match?" And she took out a cigarette to light. They looked at each other. Peter did not believe that she actually had any money. Yet he hoped. And in this hope was the same kind of feeling Vicki had been feeling for years, the feeling that a great deal of money could be hers for nothing at all.

"What do you have now?" Peter said, with some tension in his voice.

"Not a thing," she said gaily, so gaily her voice lighted the terrible circumstance and made it something else.

"Nothin?" Peter said again.

"Not a thing," Vicki said again, with an impatient feminine tone to her voice, and her eyes somewhat startled just as the wind blew. Then she held Mickey's hand as she lit a cigarette off his match and glanced over at Peter quickly.

Mickey Dunn said nothing.

Vicki noticed the huge envelope with the contract that Peter had brought over from his house. It was the contract she had signed in December. It had put a great light into her soul when she had signed it. Now, it was the black hole.

She took another drag of the cigarette and smiled and set her purse down beside it.

"I'm telling you boys I'm going to get good and drunk tonight because of this – this, boys, is my night to howl."

Both of them laughed gaily. Both knew at that second

she was lying through her teeth. Both of them understood that if Peter wanted off the hook, something else would have to be done.

Peter Bathurst walked toward the small concrete one-and-one-half-storey mall that had been built in 1980. The back of this mall had been singed by a fire started by Sylvain Gatineau at one time, angry that the mall had been built on reserve land. You could still make out the scorch marks up the side of the building. Peter entered the mall through McCaustere Gordon and McCaustere's outside office door.

Tracy McCaustere, the young woman from Shackle's Canadian Literature class, was now Peter Bathurst's lawyer. She had been his lawyer since 1989. Peter had taken his father to the bus to go and raise support for him in the south. He had tried to get in touch with an assistant deputy minister who had once told him to phone whenever he needed anything, but he could not be reached.

Now he went to see his lawyer.

He sat down in the soft chair and looked back at Tracy McCaustere as she closed the door. He looked at her expectantly. The expectant look now said this: that his life depended on something that was in her hands. It was the only time in his life he'd ever felt this, and he could not get over how terrible a feeling it was.

In former times, this office had been a sanctuary, a place where he was always welcome. This was no longer true.

However, over the last week, he had sensed this. He no longer had the feeling that he was welcome in this office.

It was as if everything in the room had shifted allegiance and was out to catch him. And the more decisive he tried to be, the more hopeless it was.

In the last hour he had also discovered to be true something he was hoping wasn't. Vicki could not get the money. Nothing made him more desperate than this fact. Now he had come to Tracy to listen to her, and to pretend.

He had needed a lawyer once for a private matter, about the house he was building, and he'd looked Tracy McCaustere up. They had been close since that time.

He glanced about, smiling when she did. He was a big man who had taken care of his whole band for years, but from now on, no one would remember what good he had done. At six o'clock they would come to his house, and by tomorrow he would be taken into custody by the RCMP. And yet he knew, deep in his heart, at the deepest part, that his accusers were as guilty as he was that the casino had failed.

If they had helped him in any way over the last three years, everything would have worked out.

He sat in the hot room staring at her and not speaking. He remembered his childhood, his and that of dozens of his friends. He could count twenty-nine of them who were now dead. And of those twenty-nine, twenty-one had either been murdered or had committed suicide. He, in his braver days, had once taken a gun out of a man's hand when the man had come into the bar.

In bygone days he had picked blueberries and potatoes and had been content. He was thinking as Tracy spoke, not listening to her. She was telling him what he already knew, about the facts surrounding the failure of the casino and the sudden insolvency of Commix, which stood for Co-operative Micmac Expertise. It was the fledgling company he had run out of the back of the band office on his own, and which Bathurst and Dunn Enterprises had billed for the last three years.

Tracy spoke as if this insolvency should be a revelation to him. And he was thinking of a small snowdrift and a rabbit that he had snared some thirty-four years ago.

She told him only what he knew. The band was going to turn the investigation over to the RCMP, unless he could account for most of the money by six o'clock. She had asked for an extension, but the Band Council felt an extension was not possible. And it was even more money than he had thought. Close to sixty thousand dollars was missing.

He glanced up at her ruefully when she said this.

For a long time he said nothing, and she waited for him to speak. He pursed his lips and breathed quietly.

Finally he spoke. He said that they should not allow RCMP on the reserve because it would violate self-government. And he sounded suddenly as if he thought this was the main point.

"If you could just tell me where you put the money – in what accounts – I'm sure we could clear it all up," Tracy said. For weeks he had been telling her that he had the money, and that all the accusations were nonsense, and that people were only out to steal this money so he had hidden it. Because for weeks he'd felt that he would still get the go-ahead for the casino, that millions of dollars could still be made.

The snow drifted down, and rested on the aluminum siding next door. And he thought of the rabbit again and how it had waited out the night in the snare.

"Money," he said, scornfully, "dat's all people ever talk about – money." And again he was emphatic when he mentioned the RCMP. That they should not be allowed on the reserve.

Tracy said nothing. She only nodded. The idea was that the ultimate truth of a situation could be chipped away at by various little truths.

"Money," he said again, and he sniffed and looked up at her. As if the main reason for Commix had not been to funnel money out of a trust fund to help him get a casino.

The rabbit, the snowdrift, and his cousin with the bright feather on his snowshoes. This was what he was thinking of.

He sniffed and looked about, as if wondering how all of this, or any of this, had happened to him. He remembered starting a company, giving money to people, and writing cheques. But what was that?

He tapped his boots and sighed. His hands were thick and his fingers rounded. Oh, he'd had terrible drunks too where he'd fought with everyone, and once he had rolled right through a fire while he was trying to choke someone. He sniffed at this memory and looked at Tracy. She wouldn't know any of this.

"The money is in a safe place – it's to be used for the environment," he said. He looked at her boldly, even angrily, because this is how a lie must be told.

"Ah – the environment," Tracy said, startled a second, and then looking at him gravely. She knew this was a lie. Neither of them spoke.

He sighed, the way people had come to expect. Just as they had come to expect anything or everything from him. Just as they had come to expect his gentleness to the elderly, and his occasional meanness to friends.

She smiled at him once again and he nodded seriously, still thinking of the rabbit.

He left the building, and the smell of workmen's mortar, and he spat. The minutes, now, were ticking away.

Now, at this second, Peter Bathurst viewed both Tracy McCaustere and Mickey Dunn as self-serving at his expense.

Yet only now, when his price had tumbled into the snow, did he realize how expensive they were going to be. He had been juggled back and forth like a magician's ball, living above others and loving the feel of the air. Sometimes treating his friends meanly. He had treated Diane Bartibog's husband LeRoy especially mean.

But now that great magician had lost his grip and it wasn't in the ball's power to get that grip back. That the magician had lost his grip came to Peter slowly, as the realization of great tragedy.

There was only one person he feared – who knew all about Commix and Dunn and Bathurst Enterprises.

Earlier today, just before he took his father to the bus station, Mickey Dunn had phoned him. He tried to convince Peter then that the casino was all Peter and Vicki Shackle's idea, and that he himself had had nothing to do with it, or the funnelling of any money from Commix.

"I did not want to tell you this before," Mickey said sadly, "but where is she? Where is her money? I mean, I spent as much as you – I might lose my bar. We knew the dangers. She wanted to be a partner though and talked you into it. I warned you not to get mixed up with her – you remember what I said? Remember I brought you into my office – remember? Remember all I said? What a loon she is – remember?"

Peter remembered nothing of this. And he had no idea where over half the money went.

Now, after three years of high living, it quite suddenly became Vicki Shackle who was responsible for it all. That poor sick woman with the haughty eyes and timid smile.

That was their new solution. When last month neither of them would have given her the time of day.

Peter turned now, and began to run, back toward the bar.

Mickey was still in the office as Peter came in and sat down again. He was throwing things around as if he had been upset for some time. He picked up his prize collection of baseball cards and rashly flung them into the air as Peter entered. Then he looked at Peter as if to say: *See? See? This has got to me too. So don't you dare accuse me of not bearing my part of the responsibility.* But Peter was in no position to say anything. Because what Peter was hoping – a far outside hope, but a hope nonetheless – was that Mickey would give him the money.

He calculated it like this: if Commix had spent fifty thousand and Mickey gave back twenty-five thousand Peter could get the rest over the next few months. Not from Vicki or Garth – he wouldn't bother them – but from those who had loitered about the Commix office when they thought it was to their benefit. He might even be able to ask Tracy McCaustere for a loan.

He had been Mickey's friend off and on for ten years. He had never asked him for a thing. Mickey had made thousands and thousands of dollars in the last ten years off illegal salmon and moose meat that they had secretly sold.

Peter took a breath and said nothing for a moment.

The bar was quiet, smelled of brass taps and beer and that particular closeness of leftover memories.

The little office was almost dark. Mickey's bulldog face had a terrible aspect. It was the face of a man who wanted rid of a responsibility over someone he had used. And that someone was Peter Bathurst. And Peter recognized this look because he had seen it when Mickey had used and had discarded others, like Sylvain Gatineau, like Garth Shackle.

Mickey also had the appearance of all men of business when the idea implicit in business, that of gaining or losing money, takes over. He had a look of wary connivance, fear and panic that made him hard to look at. The one thing Mickey had relied on was that Peter and his forces on the reserve would remain powerful, that Commix would remain solvent. Now he felt it was he who had been tricked.

Mickey felt Peter was about to ask him for money, and he braced himself for it. He turned away and began to grumble.

Peter had never in his life asked anyone for anything. He thought for a second, as a skipper might think about how best to tack a sailboat into wind.

Yet what he said was the truth. Peter said he had only managed to rob his own people.

"Dammit all – I only manage to rob my own, with Commix."

He said this in the heavy and childlike Micmac accent that had never left him. Dunn turned like a cat, jumped on this indiscreet disclosure, sensing he had found a way out for himself. If he had used any other tack, Peter may have had a chance.

"I know," Dunn said, shaking his head sadly. "It was terrible what you did. But it wasn't all your fault. It was that man from Devon's fault, too. Although everyone is responsible for themselves. That's the game. I told you about Commix. Told you that Diane's people would find out – eh? Did you listen to me? Ha ha! Didn't I? Heh-heh-heh."

He walked over and rubbed Peter's head jovially, like you would rub a child's head, and Peter stared at him in numb disbelief.

This office too had been very important to Peter. For years he had felt as comfortable here as a member of the family. He called all of Mickey's children by their pet names, remembered their birthdays, and spoke with a kind of innocent flirtatiousness with Mickey's wife.

Now suddenly he realized that everything, down to the chair he sat on, told him that he wasn't wanted here any more. Even he could feel his own presence here as a burden. The inner circle had shifted. It was miles and miles away.

"Why in God's name did you spend so much for a damn casino?" Mickey continued, as if a caution now or a lecture was what was needed. "I tried to warn you," he said, shifting his weight from one leg to the other, "I did my best – I tried." His eyes darted here and there continually. It was something he did which Peter had only noticed with others before, those sad others who were always on the outside.

"I didn't spend so much – like everyone – dat's all – why are you saying this?" he answered, suddenly frightened. But Mickey's terrible eyes fastened on him, in this little place, and Peter fell silent.

Peter then actually tried to figure out where all the money had gone. It was at this moment Peter knew that he would be blamed for everything.

Then Mickey Dunn himself had a terrible confession to make – and he bent closer to make it. He even said it as a bet as he held Peter's hand for a second. He said he bet that Peter didn't know that he himself had nothing, and owned nothing. There was a lien on the tavern and a lien on the cottage. He was the big loser here.

"I'm just as low as a nigger," he said. And then he sniffed, and his face with its flat nose looked hurt that people had always taken advantage of him. The wind blew against the window. And the idea fell like silver and gold into Peter's ear, the idea that Mickey had given his life to help him. It seemed that from his childhood until now, pure altruism was what had been going on, on his part, and everyone had taken advantage of him. The old tattoo of a crown sat faded on Mickey's arm.

Then he began to pace, moving one heavy leg in front of the other, and walking with his hands behind his back, as a general might who was oppressed by the idea of sending men into battle.

His house was in his wife's name, and she wanted a separation. He glanced over at Peter and glanced away. So nothing was his. Glanced, glanced away. His wife would be the one to walk away from this with everything. Glanced, glanced. And quite sadly he began to talk of his love for his daughter, "Puppsa-Wuppsa." He paused for effect, and then continued. He had given his daughter everything, "the best education," as he put it, and now she thought she was too good for him, had a friend who was a classical guitarist and who couldn't do anything because he might bruise a stupid finger. Mickey laughed at this, and looked at Peter as if he should laugh also. Peter had heard this same anecdote last year. At that time, however, Mickey was filled with a trembling, sentimental admiration for the stout-faced classical guitarist, who couldn't pick up a string bean for fear of bruising a finger.

"He's not like you and me, Peter," Mickey had said, tearfully.

But now the classical guitarist had become another casualty of the terrible day.

It was as if, in the coddled storm, the world was disappearing.

Peter could not ask for money now, and Mickey sensed this.

"Here," Mickey said now, suddenly holding out his arm with the violent passion he always showed. "Cut it off – that's what I can offer."

Peter's mouth began to tremble just slightly. He said he didn't want to cut the arm off, Mickey knew that. But his mouth trembled only because he had seen Mickey do this with others – the endlessly disposable ones, like poor Sylvain Gatineau.

The reserve was a horror and Peter had wanted to change it, but like so many other men he had managed to use this horror for his own benefit. That's what people did. They just left the horror behind. For implicit in changing it was changing it to match his own dreams, coming from his own tormented soul. Bingo games and a casino.

When Peter came in, Vicki had been playing the machines far at the back. Now Peter stood and went to the door.

The tavern was almost dark.

"Vick," he said. "Vicki."

He looked toward her favourite machine. The machine she came to play at six o'clock at night when other mothers in town were busy with their children or their husbands.

Peter walked toward it slowly, trying in the dim bar to make her out. He would have to get some money from her, this was imperative now.

Four loonies and a burning cigarette sat upon the machine. Her coat draped over the chair. But she was gone.

"You'll have to find her," Dunn said. "I think she's taken that envelope with your contract." Then pausing he added, "You're in deep trouble now."

Suddenly the idea was this: Mickey Dunn was no longer a part of this trauma, but simply a spectator, sadly offering advice.


Mickey Dunn went into the office again and washed his hands. His office was dark and littered, and smelled of old cologne and leather. It was said that he had robbed his brother of his brother's wife. It was said – well, everything was said. In the back room – that is the pine room behind the office – was where he sold moose and salmon, and bear paws, and shipped bear gall bladders off to Asia.

The old tavern was slanted and shook in the storm. More than one government official, member of the Power Commission, deputy minister had come through those doors to get illegal salmon. The Shackles had fought against this for years.

There was a storm forever in Mickey Dunn's heart. A storm, they said, for stealing his younger brother's wife. A storm because his daughter, whom he called "Puppsa-Wuppsa," had gone to university and had found herself reading about her father in Dexter's second novel. She had come back to the village one night in the dark, and he was having his nap on the leather couch in the office – for he rarely went home. He woke to feel her presence. She was sitting in the dark, smoking, and looking at him.

"Hi, hon," he said, and yet at that moment, he knew – she knew. She knew about Dexter's novel, and had recognized him in it.

She sat there all that night. The curtains blew, as a sigh, revealing her sorrow for him, and his sorrow too, and the sorrow of the world, as his dark brooding eyes flashed in the wind.

Today, he felt a little sorry for Peter Bathurst and his simple-minded trust of the Devon man. His funny little company Commix, which Mickey always called Comic for a joke. All the squaws gave him money, to help them build a day-care. That wasn't so cute.

He could understand why the band had turned against Peter Bathurst. Why some were even plotting to kill him. He, Mickey, wouldn't have been so trusting with people. And then he grinned.

Indians were really quite funny.

He rubbed his flat face with his flat hand and went and lay on the couch again. He felt sorry for the Indians and how they got in such mix-ups. Commix was one big example. But some of the mix-ups were quite funny. He yawned and closed his eyes, and cleared his throat. Yes, they had pretty funny mix-ups some times, he thought.

He forgot the part he had played in his friend's downfall. Well, in fact, in purely business terms he needed Peter to fail now, so he could start to deal with others. If there was to be a casino he could supply all the tables, and a lot of the expertise. But whatever it was to be, he would be there. Maybe a big bingo hall smack in the centre of the reserve.

Mickey was five-foot-five, overweight, and always wore a huge cowboy belt and high leather boots with "M.D." on them. He went to truck pulls across the States every February.

He looked like a huge baby as he went from one table to another in the tavern, talking over local politics. He owned three apartment buildings, four warehouses, and a tire store. He was forever snapping gum, and people said you had to watch him if he ever started to blow bubbles, because that meant he would grab a tire iron.

At the same time he controlled many small and terrible lives about him. That was what his favourite daughter had found out about him through Dexter's second book.

What no one knew, no one at all, was that Vicki had paid him twelve hundred dollars in secret, for the chance to sign the contract to be a partner.

To Vicki, her beauty gone, her husband no longer in love with her, her dreams as faded as her looks, playing poker machines with money she had stolen from Pumpkin, it was everything she had left. It had been the most important moment of her life in the last five years. It was her last chance to get everything back for her and Garth, to make him proud of her once again. She had believed in the casino like someone might believe in a gold rush. She was like a woman of fifty finally going back to work again. It was a hope like that – sacrilegious to dash. She was so stunned by the amount she owed now, so remorseful of all the trouble she had caused, that she had been foolish enough to try to run away. But where could she run today in a storm?

If one ever mentioned her poignant dream to Mickey – made more poignant by her years of selfishness – he would look at him mystified and hurt that he would ever blame him for destroying it. He had only done all he could do to help another human being on the journey through life. Now that she had to pay twenty thousand and had not even seen a poker chip, that was not his fault. That was business. The word *business* was most often mentioned when people destroyed someone's life at business.

Besides, as he loosened his belt in the half-dark room and rubbed his hand over his flat face again, *he knew, he knew, he knew* – he couldn't help it.

In some ways he was not only loved, he was revelled in. People spoke about knowing Mickey Dunn, about being his friend.

"You might know Mickey – but no one understands Mickey like me –" is what Vicki used to say.

"No, darlin, I understand him more betterer than you," Garth would answer. While Pumpkin, sitting between them would look at one and then the other.

He was, in his own uncouth way, a darling, very much like and very much greater than Professor Wheem, and Vicki Shackle was the one who would understand.

He knew that when he held out his arm and, misty-eyed, told people to cut it off, there was always a chance someone would.

When Vicki got outside she drove about and then pulled into a parking lot to think. But the more she thought the more she began to tremble. She could not stop. She did not like to go about town trembling like a leaf – but for the last week this was what she had done. Besides, now she didn't have her coat.

Now she was hiding in the back seat of her car, with the seat blanket over her.

"I'll stay here for a week or so," she thought.

For the last three months she had been filled with the hope of a child, and now it had all evaporated.

She hated what she was remembering at this moment: "I'm allowing you in on this one," Mickey had told her, "because I like you – I always have liked you – not because I owe you one red cent –" And Vicki had smiled, had become almost hilarious when she signed the contract. She remembered the night air. The sparkling wine. The idea of the bar.

"I don't mind you in on this," he said. "But I don't want every Tom, Dick, and Harry in on this."

"There won't be, there won't be – Mickey, there won't be."

"Well, I've always been a big sucker for ya, is what I've been."

"I know, Mickey, I know, Mickey, I know – I know –"

"Don't go about blabbin this to Garth – yet."

The car windows were covered in snow, and etched with ice. When she had read Narnia to Pumpkin, she had always been so frightened of the White Witch. But it was what poor Pumpkin called her by the time she turned six.

No one could see into the car today. Sometimes people passed so close she could hear them breathe as they walked by.

Garth had gone over to see Mickey about the twenty thousand a week ago. He wanted to find out exactly what the contract stipulated and if they would drag Vicki into court. Vicki was at home lying on the couch, bawling her eyes out.

"I'm too busy to see you," Mickey had said, coming out of the back room, and then turning and going back inside.

Garth had waited in the outer office on the leather couch for three hours, as Mickey paced back and forth in the other room, now and then looking out at him.

Then in the late afternoon Garth had hobbled back across the bridge. Vicki had watched him coming across the bridge, from the upstairs window.

"I bet they never were our friends," he said.

"Shhh," Vicki said. "We'll be okay."

"No!" Garth exclaimed over and over. "We have to protect Pumpkin – she's the only thing we ever had. What have we done to her?"

They then looked down over the small yard, the outbuildings, and slabs of snow, and were quiet. Both of them looked and felt like children who had been caught at something bad that they had unintentionally done.

Garth said he would not pay. He would not phone Verriker, or ask old Tom. Vicki took his hand and told him they would simply burn the house to the ground.

"Who told you they would do something like that?" he said.

"I read it," she said, "when I went to university, in a book." And she took a drag off her cigarette and looked away.

Garth for the first time in months seemed rejuvenated. He ate breakfast, he hobbled about the house. He said he would not pay – anything. He'd send Pumpkin away, to Vancouver, where he had some hockey friends. No one would ever bother them again. Vicki had begged him to contact his friends to help pay the money back. Former hockey friends. Just this one more time.

Garth had refused.

He had refused her for the very first time in his life. He phoned Verriker and told him not to send a dime.

He had bought a ticket for Pumpkin.

But Pumpkin refused to leave.

How could she go, if her father was so sick?

It was now one-forty-five on Holy Thursday afternoon.

Peter Bathurst thought that if it was last month, or last year, he would let it all go – but now? Now things were different. Now the election had come and gone. And now they had his account numbers. He felt that he must try to save face. He did not want to be a scapegoat for those who would profit from his downfall. Especially LeRoy Penniac.

The snow came down and he went into a field of pit-props, and sat on a butt of pulp, with his back nestled against the logs.

He stared at his boots, and at his hands. His hands were deep brown and really quite masterful at fixing appliances.

Then thinking things over he stood, brushed the snow away, and walked to the band office. He went inside and sat on an auditorium chair in the corner.

LeRoy, Diane Bartibog's husband, was at the desk but Peter did not acknowledge him. He scratched his face and pretended to be deep in thought about some unrelated matter. LeRoy had been the one to accuse Peter of firing through Diane Bartibog's window with a 30.30 during the election. In fact, almost everyone believed he had done it.

There was only one other person in the office – the large-breasted secretary with the placid face, She did not look Peter's way, although three months ago she would have done anything for him. This slight was the most painful. Peter kept looking at her, but she kept her eyes averted.

The air smelled sweet and hot. LeRoy now sat at the desk with the box. He took a key from his pocket, a key that had once belonged to Peter, as if the key was the most important symbol in the world.

Then he unlocked the box and took out some money. It was as if money was nothing. Not to those who had the keys, who had the accounts. And that was the main point. It wasn't. The secretary went on with her work.

LeRoy looked Peter's way and smiled slightly. It was the same smile Peter had used with others, three or four years before. It was a whimsical smile revealing mastery. LeRoy took twenty, perhaps twenty-two thousand dollars from that box. They didn't ask him where he'd got it. Then speaking in Micmac to the secretary he asked her if Sergeant Delano had phoned. The secretary said no. Finally she glanced Peter's way.

Peter asked where Diane was, and neither answered him. They only glanced at one another.

He then spoke. He declared that bringing the RCMP onto the reserve was a violation of self-government. He tried to sound very indignant. He then said that Diane had a white father – Reggie Shackle – which was probably why she liked the RCMP. Again they said nothing.

So he sat there, and smoked a cigarette.

He sighed, and looked out the window, with the cigarette pinched in his fingers. "How long do you think it will snow?" he asked no one in particular.

"Long time," he answered himself.

Of course, as he left the band office he knew where that twenty-two thousand dollars that LeRoy played with had come from.

It had been taken from the accounts and added to the money they now said Peter had misappropriated from the band. And it would be very hard for him to prove this, because no one knew that he hadn't taken it except for him and LeRoy himself.

He suddenly decided to leave the town. And all his plans were now focused on this. He walked back across town toward the bank. There was a teller he knew at the bank who would look up Vicki's account number, and tell him what she had. He had done this before.

But when he got to the bank the woman wasn't there. He cursed slightly.

He thought then that he might still have some money left himself.

Inside the bank at the teller machine, he took out his blue card. Now *everything* bothered and pained him. The smell of the bank, the slips of paper from the machine lying on the floor. The card which had once brought him so much indifferent happiness simply lay flat and undignified in his hand. And when he punched in three hundred dollars, the screen showed insufficient funds. He turned, without bothering to take his card, and left the bank.

He would always remember how the door creaked behind him and how he had turned. He would remember this always. For if he hadn't turned – if he had just walked across the street as he had intended to do – everything would have happened differently that day.

Behind the bank, standing in the snow and drinking a bottle of Hermit wine, was Louis Gatineau. The snow came down, the flakes wet and sleepy and large.

Louis was actually on his way to help at the barn, and then to go to Campbellton and see his grandmother. When it came down to it he did not want to leave Pumpkin in the lurch.

"Have you seen Vicki Shackle?" Peter asked suddenly. He was not going to ask this. In fact he almost didn't. It was asked because the way Louis tipped his bottle of wine reminded him of the way Vicki had tipped a beer the night she had signed the contract.

"No – I haven't seen her since yesterday – she was playing the machine at the grocery store – do you want to go there?"

"See if you can find her," Bathurst said, and he looked down over the hill at the bloated snow, the river turning away into the distance. "I want to talk to her." He was thinking of nothing more than asking Vicki for enough money to leave the province. But like most people who had to get away, he had nowhere else to go.

Louis turned and left him, and Bathurst was alone.

The small bus that ran this route had gone off the road at one-forty-five. It had smashed through a guardrail and had broken off some boughs as it tumbled over a hill, its hood flipping open. It ended up against a tree that saved it from a twenty-five-foot drop to the river below.

A few of the passengers were hurt and could not go anywhere. Yet not another car, not even a transport truck, passed on the road.

The bus driver had left to get help and had not come back. And now everyone was anxious, thinking he had got lost in the storm, though they tried to make the best of it. The worst case of injury was a man with a swollen ankle who refused to stop trying to walk. He hopped from one seat to another, up and down the aisle, though people told him to be careful.

"I think it's okay – no no no – I think it is."

"How's your ankle?" Tom asked.

"I think she's okay." And he smiled as if his problem was the one that was meant to entertain everyone.

"Don't move – don't move – the bus might go down," someone shouted.

And some of them burst out laughing.

Professor Wheem sat on the inside seat three-quarters of the way back, on the right. Now and then he put his hand on the seat in front of him, as if deciding to stand. But then he did not. He had taken his scarf off and had it wrapped about his ears, because he was cold.

*It's easy enough for them*, he thought. *I have a committee meeting today – dammit*. And he decided that if he didn't have a committee meeting he wouldn't be afraid.

*Well, dammit – I'll be damned if I'll sit here taking this*, he thought, for effect.

He looked about, as if someone else knew what he was thinking.

He was very angry, but no one on the bus would have any idea why. No one here would have heard or have cared very much about a writer named Wheem.

Finally Wheem got up and moved along the tilted bus aisle. He moved past everyone with an "excuse me" as polite as he could muster, and stepped off the bus as if he were doing something no one thought him capable of doing. But hardly anyone paid attention to him. Only the man with the tall fur hat, like a French hussar, looked out the window and nodded.

"Going to cap a well?" he asked.

"Pardon me?" Wheem said.

"Taking a piss?"

"No – not at all," Wheem said. But he didn't know whether or not to laugh.

"Well, you better watch where ya step," he said, nodding. And Wheem noticed he was four or five feet closer to the slope than he had thought.

Far below, the river turned and twisted under its three feet of dark grey ice, and from somewhere to somewhere a small bird flitted.

Wheem started toward the road, but the going was difficult, even in the bough-strewn wake of the bus, and he found himself floundering up to his waist in snow. Halfway up the hill his feet were soaking and he was shivering, and he sat on a stump.

Now it felt like night. But at any given moment someone might come by and he would still be able to make it – he would be late for the meeting and the party after, but only fashionably so.

"Where were you?"

"I was in a bus accident, dammit!"

And he would relate the story about the man with the hussar hat and the old Indian who had white hair as fine as a spider web down his back.

Yet he didn't want to go on by himself. He would pay someone to go on with him.

He had been sweating and now he was cold – but he did not want to go back to the bus – it was too far down the hill; he could hear better from up here if a car were to come by or the bus driver were to come back.

He looked at his big gloves and slapped his knees with them as if he was sitting at Le Chateau.

And then he looked up and saw the little man who had first nodded to him in the bus station.

The little man nodded, bent over and lit a cigarette, turning his back to the wind, and puffed on it, with it tilted in the air.

"There we go, boy – how's she goin?" he said.

"I'm fine," Wheem said, and for a second his face took on the appearance of a mask that was always hidden by his goatee and harmless-looking eyes.

"Boys, that's some jeesless bad storm right there now – but I look at her this way – we coulda went off the road on the other side of her – and if we hadda done that, none of us'd be complainin, mister man – there's a fifty-foot drop down to the river on the other side of er. No tree to save us there."

The little man kept fidgeting. In his snow-slicked jeans with their big cuffs he looked like a wrinkled boy of about seventy-five. His hat was pulled down to his ears. His nose was flat and red: "Bashed her in, at a fight in Sunny Corner." As he said.

He had one thumb missing.

The worst of it was, he kept talking, and Wheem looked like he did at poetry readings when a poet of greater ability than himself read. His face took on the appearance of self-torment, reserved for himself whenever he couldn't lash out and bully.

The old man talked about his son, who was dying. Who drank wine and beer all his life.

"Wallowed about in pity like a pig." Who could lift a three-hundred-pound tractor axle. Whose kidneys were now gone. Who took heart pills because his heart had been bruised in a hockey game, years and years ago, and now his liver was gone because of those very pills he took for his heart. In terrible pain, his son limped or crawled about the house, and for almost a year had hidden like a turtle from most people, except for a little "retarder" boy he loved, and used to tickle.

The old man said he would meet his son in the middle of the night crawling here or there about the house. " 'You in pain, boy?' 'N'tall –' 'Why are you all writhing about like a worm on the floor?' 'I like doing it –'

"Sometimes it took him thirty minutes to get to the flush," he said.

This was the painful, depressing story Wheem was supposed to listen to.

"What did he do?" Wheem asked.

"He was one of the greats in hockey – one of the greats, though no one has heard a word about him in years. His wife did some articles on him with a professor guy – fictioned it up."

And Tom smiled at this, and looked at his cigarette glowing weakly beneath the tree in the grey afternoon.

Then he came over and sat down not far from Wheem, as if Wheem wanted him to continue.

Wheem now felt a terrible nakedness and emptiness wash over him.

"Your son is dying?"

Wheem's first concern was how it would affect him, and the articles he had done. And if he who was so considerate could ever be blamed in any way.

"He should be dead already," Tom answered, as if this suddenly made himself more important, and contemplating the cigarette's wet paper he took a draw.

"He would have been dead already to please her. He went from one team to the other – each team gettin worse – each road trip getting longer – each year playing hurt, with busted ribs, pukin blood. He wrassled – called himself the Shackle Tackle – member?" Tom brightened up: "Fought the Stomper at Moncton."

But Wheem until this moment was unaware of this, or that Garth had become a "wrassler."

"He could wrassle," Tom said, and he butted his cigarette in the snow. He stood and walked away from Wheem, and with his back turned unzipped his zipper, glancing back now and again over his shoulder.

"He could wrassle – he wrassled in Lorneville and over in Maine – he was a good enough wrassler – but there was no money in it, and in the end he went back to hockey – though he could hardly skate."

He turned, zipped up his zipper, and coming back to sit down added with finality: "But she was like the secretary over at the panelboard plant – she loved the bosses. And he wasn't no boss. I think she was mildly mixed up with her professor."

"Do you have anyone else?" Wheem asked quickly.

"I have a boy who *is* a professor – just about the smartest lad in the world, I do suppose – always phonin me, you know, asking if he can do anything for us – do anything for us – do anything – and I got a boy Reginald in the army – he's far away in Bosnia over at that place now – so he's not so smart, I do suppose."

The snow came down over the earth, down and down and down over the gloomy trees in back of them, where now and then a small sifting sound came to Wheem's ear.

"After she done those articles with the big-feelin lad – I don know why – everyone called her a bitch back home, and she come home with nothin – and Garthy was broken to bits fighting for her – always fighting for her – in lonely places – always alone against lads who'd torment her. He had to fight them. There was no one else to take her side."

"What happened to her?" Wheem said uncomfortably.

"You could not look at her without knowing she was a angel – a angel –" Tom turned. "She was a fallen angel, her shorts half a way up her beautiful arse." He looked away. "After she came home, she had to get all the money back – and then – the sharks came – the sharks." Wheem thought Tom meant sharks in the symbolic sense, but Tom naively meant it more as an aphorism. "They came and took her money, for gambling debts and everything, the poor godforsaken little thing, and I remortgaged the house – now, a few months ago she tried to get in on the casino – you musta heard about the casino. All the fights going on about it here these last three years. There were seven partners, and she was one. Now her partners say she owes money, to pay back on the investment. Guilt can only go – only go so far."

"Is your son at the hospital?" Wheem said, frightened.

"We've been trying to get him to go to the hospital for five months. It's always, 'I'll go tomorrow.' He'll never go. Too proud."

Wheem went to the doctor for every ache and imagined pain. And he did not understand this at all. Wheem stood up and brushed off his pants, contemplating what to say. These were her people. The people she had spoken to him about. The people that he had always considered subhuman.

And now at this moment he got an inkling of her, with them. Old Tom looked up at him and blinked kindly, as he had done all his life to everyone.

"I can't help them no more," Tom said. And just as he had smiled readily, just as readily as that, a tear came to his eye.

There was a long pause. The day darkened in the corners. Their little world seemed still.

"Vicki – the real truth about Vicki is this – you can't stop love."

"Love – you mean with her professor friend?" Wheem asked.

"No, sir – I don't mean with her professor – no sirree – I

mean with the man she married – the man who spit in her
face – I mean the man who slapped her – I mean love, you
can't stop love. Nothing else. For HIM. For HIM. Love."
He sniffed like a Philosophy major at this statement and
there was something wretched about it.

"And yet," Tom continued, "what did he do for love?
He broke every bone in his body, and for love of country
he ruined his chance at a career in Boston. For love of her
and Pumpkin he wrassled in front of fat women in
Neguac." And he sniffed again.

"For love of him she came home from university and
took a job as salesgirl, and made plans to get their money
back – and gambled for years to get their money back.
Love – can't stop it."

All Vicki's vanity (actually the only thing Wheem was
attracted to) disappeared, and to him there was, now in
the snow, something mystical about her. Something finer
in her search for money than Wheem had ever imagined.

"So what will happen to them now?" Wheem said, pretending to feign interest, when this question was actually
the most important he had ever asked.

"Oh, they will die," Tom said. "They will die – just like
my old blind old horse – they will die – both of them have
been wanting to DIE for twenty years. And I love them
more than life – but I'm too old. I can't pay off any more
debts or warn them about any more people. Both of them
are children, you see. That's why I love them so much."

He looked at his hand with the missing thumb and said
nothing else. Only Wheem thought this conversation

incidental, and that the old man did not know who he was, or whom he had seen that morning.

For a second Wheem thought he had done something terrible, but then he was relieved to think it was something he was bound to get away with.

He forgot now that he had thought earlier in the day that God calls on man not to be comfortable but to be great.

The old man stood. His jeans took on the colour of the trees, a deep, deep blue. His hat was old and bent. His face had a hundred marks on it, every groove testifying to some disappointment.

Wheem's face showed itself in the half-dark, and each day, anywhere he was, once the day ended, it was a face that had betrayed itself.

The last time he had been in the woods – though he was not really in the woods now, he only presumed he was – the last time was when he was a counsellor at summer camp in Ontario. He was eighteen. It came back to him now in startling images as the wind blew.

Wheem had ingratiated himself with another camp counsellor – a rich boy, whose father owned a tobacco farm.

He had followed the rich boy about, in that dreary fly-wasted place in Ontario, the small white-faced hopeless children of poor moms and dads who had deserted them in the summer heat as much out of love and longing for them to be in the company of proper boys like Wheem as anything else.

It was startling, too, how they began to tease the children, and make them do tasks. One, an overprotected boy with a limp, Wheem especially went after.

Who led whom – he or the rich boy – this was a question that could not be answered. They were bored. So they put the boys in a shale pit wearing only their underwear and threw soccer balls at their heads as the boys tried in vain to get out. The pit was always just a little too deep, and when the tougher boys managed to grope their way to the top, Wheem's shoe was always there to push them back down. He thought it was actually very funny.

One little boy protested, trying to protect the boy with the limp: "We could get a lawyer."

"My dad has more money than lawyers," the rich boy said, a handsome, too-clever, thin-waisted boy, with impeccable slacks and running shoes, impeccable golfing habits, incredible talents. He had been to dinner where Lester Pearson spoke.

They went home.

It seemed to have been forgotten about. That is, not until Wheem had to go to court. There to testify against him in the stern meaningless courtroom, a place where guilt or innocence could be assessed but forgiveness never granted, was the rich boy, with his father's lawyer, and the children, all the sad youngsters who had gone away to camp.

The rich boy did not look at him, looked instead to his own father and his lawyer, and smiled. Wheem's parents didn't take the time to come to court. They and everyone had let him down.

It was at this point that he had given up chances for university in Toronto, and came east – where now, twenty-seven years later, he was sitting in a thicket of snow and wild timber with Tom Shackle, the father-in-law of the woman he had used.

He had heard one thing about the Shackles from Emile Dexter that long-ago night when Dexter threatened him: "Don't you understand?" Dexter had said. "Their country has betrayed them all. Just like the Micmacs they live beside."

Peter was in his house, upstairs where he kept his rifles. He sat on his bed looking over at St. Brenden's. The air was still.

He was waiting for his father to telephone from the other reserve. He should have been there by now. Peter was sweating even though it was cool. He had his bag packed, but he had no money to go anywhere.

Maybe everything would resolve itself magically, and once it did he would be able to look back on this moment with a good deal of humour. He wiped his face with his hand. He remembered the man he had taken the gun from in the bar. The man had come into the bar that night to shoot Mickey but he couldn't get the barrel turned toward him.

Mickey was watching them wrestle, saying: "The crazy little bastard – get him, Peter." And then he went and stood behind the coat rack, and from behind the coat rack, so that you could only see the sleeves of a coat, said again: "Get him, Peter."

The man had lost his house to Mickey in a business venture over pallets. His wife, who had left him, hung out at the bar.

"C'mon, Peter," Mickey said. "Get him, boys." Waving his hand for others to join in. "Get him, boys."

And when Peter had finally wrestled the man to the ground Mickey went over and kicked him: "Don't you ever – ever – ever come into – this bar – again – and put – on the big – show or you will – deal with – Mickey Dunn."

Peter looked out again at St. Brenden's. It looked as if it was far away on a television screen. In the distance mills spread out from the south and east – far off in Brickton he could see the flumes of fire on cold days, as brilliant as a torch. St. Brenden's sat as cold as a prisoner's wall. He had not been to church in years. But last year when Jenna Wheem thought her son Hector was going to die, they asked everyone to go to the church and pray to St. Jude. Peter Bathurst went there to pray, to save Hector Wheem, the little boy who'd always run up to people, patting them on the back at the arena during hockey games.

He watched those flumes of fires from the two mills, and he thought suddenly of suicide. It would be easy – people he knew had done it, and perhaps it was the best way, after all. Instead of running any more he could put the gun to his throat. He would betray life in this way – the life that had pissed in the face of his race for four hundred years.

Then he thought of how his poor old mother would find him. He even thought of the blood – and then suddenly he thought of Dexter's third novel. Wasn't there a suicide in that book? And hadn't they all told Dexter he was a liar for writing it? Well, then, there would be no suicide by him.

The real secret was that he felt betrayed. It wasn't the money that they wanted back, it was really his destruction that they craved. It had nothing much to do with anything but power. Nor did they even know why they wished to destroy him, or what it was about him they wanted destroyed.

Over forty thousand and a casino for the reserve, which three years ago everyone had been applauding him for, buying him drinks.

When everything started to backfire two years ago, he had tried various ways to make it work, but once the machinery failed he could not get it to work again. Over the last few months he had been in a deep depression because of it.

Now with his huge beer gut, his hands unsteady, he felt cheated by his very gregariousness and kindheartedness. Which everyone, Indians and whites, had once loved, and in which he had embraced them all.

He waited in dead silence by the telephone. Not only his father, but Tracy McCaustere had told him she would telephone if she got any word. But he had also told her that he would have the money today.

The snow came down over St. Brenden's. When Peter was growing up here, the priest wouldn't allow him to speak Micmac; and then he went to school far away near

Moncton. No matter what they did to him, he took it in stride, and laughed at it. It was one way to exist.

And then there was a plane ride and he found himself in Quebec, where he was not allowed to speak English.

It was at the time the Canadian flag was changing. And someone told him there would be a flag with a feather on it. Still he had made it back to the reserve.

And now he was waiting, for the phone to ring.

He did not know that from one-forty-nine p.m. the lines were down.

The reason he'd always disliked LeRoy Penniac was because he was a snitch for the priests. Was because he'd married Mary Francis, whom Peter loved, and then had left her when she got old, for Diane.

This was the reason, the *real* reason, Peter and Diane were on opposite sides of the casino question.

Each snowflake fell, creating its own vision of the world. Behind St. Brenden's, in the parking lot, a number of boys were playing road hockey.

Tracy had not phoned.

It was well after two.

Peter left the house, leaving a loaded 30.30 long-barrel Marlin on the bed.

So the snow came down and filled in the tire marks on the street as he walked past St. Brenden's.

The reserve looked empty. The flat windows were dark and cold. At almost every house dogs lay under the porches or came out to sniff. Now and then a car went by.

As he turned up a side street, he saw Louis Gatineau

approaching with his head down. He didn't want to speak to the boy at this moment.

To escape him there was only one place to go, and he ran through the parking lot to the back of St. Brenden's.

The church was empty. The windows were covered for Good Friday. The cross was covered, too, but the nuns had made a mistake and had left the feet of Jesus bare. From habit, Peter genuflected and took some holy water.

There was no one else here. He went to a pew and sat.

He brushed the snow off of his coat quickly and looked about. He smiled to himself about something, and then blessed himself and knelt down. And then he said one or two prayers under his breath, for Gregory Pie, his little cousin.

Everything at St. Brenden's smelled of plaster and dry and musty garments in cloistered cabinets made of pine.

He got up suddenly when he heard someone in the vestry and started to leave. Then he saw Mary Francis through a side door carting a table downstairs. His heart suddenly leapt with hope. She would at least have money enough for him to leave town.

He went through the side door and quietly down the cement steps and watched her for a moment.

The church was empty but tonight there would be Mass. People would be doing their Easter duties, and asking forgiveness, and afterwards there was the Catholic Women's League meeting and Mary Francis was getting ready for this. Later today she would have a little celebration for the children.

The huge old church was attached on one side to the rectory by a corridor lined with fonts and statues of Mary and Joseph, a large painting done after the Second World War of St. Jerome beating his breast with a rock. It all smelled so secretive.

Mary Francis turned, saw him, and smiled.

Suddenly and quite quickly he was confessing everything to her. He told her of the impending investigation and of all the good work he had tried to do; he wanted everyone to be happy. But now they were violating Indian self-government by bringing police onto the reserve to investigate him. He was very hurt by this.

Yet in the midst of his explanation came the terrible realization, because of her kind face, that he was trapped. Not only that he was trapped, but that Commix had taken $427.34 from her three months ago, as a donation toward a day-care centre. He had forgotten all about this.

"If," he said quietly in Micmac, "you have any control over money – anything at all – I could use it."

"I thought you were doing very well," she said simply.

He said that Diane Bartibog had asked yesterday that the former treasurer emphatically disclose where certain money had gone.

"Who is the former treasurer?" Mary asked.

He said nothing for a long time, and then he whispered, "I am."

"Well, then, you can go and get the money back," she said, smiling.

"I don't have the money," he said. "It's gone – I wanted to build a casino – something for everyone! As sure as I'm here they will build it for themselves – and take all the credit – and I'll get nothing. And then they will accuse me of what they themselves profit on."

He seemed very distraught by the idea of getting nothing. He felt he had worked too hard to come away with nothing.

"I don't have any money," Mary said, still smiling simply, and she put her hand on his arm. "Stay tonight in here – things look bad now. If you go outside you'll get in some more trouble."

He once loved her, when he was very young, long ago. But she was then married to LeRoy Penniac.

She had almost faltered, one evening on the river when they were alone – but then she had whispered: "No –" It was from then on that he wished to prove himself to her.

For the last twenty years he thought he was proving himself. The more powerful he became the more obscure she did and the more he believed she would love him. Then LeRoy left her for Diane, and she was alone. Peter pretended he did not care, but at almost every moment he thought of her.

"I trusted them," he said. "I trusted Mickey Dunn. I didn't do anything wrong –" And this feeling was overwhelming, that he had not really done anything wrong, but now he would go to jail. And guilt or innocence had nothing to do with it.

"I trusted, too," Mary said, smiling again. "I trusted

my husband." And she gave a quick apologetic laugh and blinked.

Here Mary was, her Sacred Heart pin attached to her worn blouse. The warm church basement had the scent of flowers and palm leaves left over from Palm Sunday.

Lent – Mary had given up chocolate, except she had backslid twice, once on her forty-second birthday, and once when she went to the drugstore and saw chocolate-covered almonds under glass.

Last year she had received an honorary doctorate from the university where Neil Shackle taught, for her tireless work with children.

These children had made crafts and small statues to sell to the tourists, and Peter had sold them for her, through his small company, Commix. This was part of the money, children's money, that was now lost along with the $427.34. She never mentioned this.

She had no solace to offer him because he was asking her to help him escape the truth. The truth was that the money was gone, he had taken it, and this is what was terrible for him to admit.

"Tracy McCaustere knows I am telling the truth," he said. "She always protected the natives – always!"

"The truth in everything is by faith, not by law," Mary said.

He had never heard her speak like this before. He knew it wasn't faith in any one church she was speaking of, it was simply faith. She herself did not so much believe in any one church as she believed that all the misery her people had suffered was for some purpose. That it had to be.

"If God does not care for me or my two children, there must be some good reason even for this."

He saw her innocent face, her strong arms, her jeans cuffed at the bottom, her fine pointed leather shoes. Everything she had ever owned was a donation from somewhere. She had never taken a cent that wasn't hers. She thought that when he started Co-operative Micmac Expertise it would allow some of the children to earn a little bit. He hadn't thought of how significant this was to her little group until now.

And here he was asking her for money.

Snow fell suddenly from the roof. She turned slightly and glanced up, and then looked back at him and smiled.

"If you stay here, things will not get any worse," she said.

It was fine for her to say. But at every step of his life a man like Peter felt that he must do something more. That was what someone like Mary Francis did not comprehend, he supposed.

If only it was last month – last year – he would have been able to stop, to go back, to re-evaluate. But now – now there was no way. If for nothing else, he had to save face for Mary. Besides, those against him – Diane Bartibog – would not stop either. And that was the problem. In fact those people, his enemies for the last three years, would benefit from any confession he made.

And he left the church and went out into the snow.

It was not his guilt that bothered him.

Many people believe that it is guilt that plagues people when, in most cases, even in cases of murder, it is their feelings of innocence. And this was what he felt now. He felt used by everyone. He thought of LeRoy, the former altarboy and snitch for the priests, counting the money from the box; he heard Mickey Dunn's voice. He remembered the dozens of times everything had almost worked only to be stopped by a vote, and he bitterly turned toward the liquor store with his last ten dollars, to find himself a drink.

Louis Gatineau had been trudging over town for some great purpose, although he had no idea what this purpose was. So he had stopped and bought another quart of wine.

He had woken this morning as always in his small trailer, which had some torn insulation on the window and some boxes placed in the centre of the floor. He had frozen most of the winter, sitting alone day and night. Then he had been hired to turn out the horses when Garth Shackle got sick. Pumpkin was always there and he fell for her. He tried to impress her. But he never seemed able to say or do anything right.

One day he had tried clumsily to tell her about his people's history. Pumpkin had told him she didn't know anything about their history, but she was sorry. She was sorry if his people had suffered, and she said what she felt was true, that most whites were sorry that his people had suffered.

Louis then asked her if she thought he was dangerous.

And she said that she didn't think he was. But since his father drank Lysol and had killed himself, Louis sometimes felt he was the most dangerous person to be around.

And so he had told Pumpkin that she had better hide the Lysol when he was near. Once he'd picked up the diesel that was used for the small tractor, and had tried to take a gulp.

"A good drink a diesel never hurt anyone," he had said. Pumpkin had spent an hour or more talking him out of it. And of course he liked her to worry and fuss over him.

Now he walked about the town drinking wine. If he had not met Peter Bathurst when he had, he would have been on his way to the train station to visit his sick old grandmother in the hospital in Campbellton. He had planned to do this, but instead he was looking for Vicki Shackle like Peter had asked. He was not sure why, but thought it must be about the gunshot that had been fired at Diane Bartibog's house, and had wounded a little girl.

Everyone was up in arms about it. The investigation was in gear, so it would be tremendously significant if he, Louis Gatineau, a nobody, brought her to justice. From far, far away the smell of the mill drifted toward him in the snow.

He lived alone in his trailer. No one paid attention to him except for Mary Francis and Peter Bathurst. Once, when he was fourteen, he had run away to live in the back of a car after his father had threatened him with a hatchet. It was not a big car but a Volkswagen, with the engine taken out. It hadn't been that big a hatchet.

The Volkswagen was at the dump, far at the back with the refrigerators, so he didn't get many visitors. Once or twice his father would come by to ask him for money.

"I'm sorry I threw a hatchet at you – give me some money."

"I don't have no money."

"When I was your age I had some spunk – I wasn't stuck in a Volkswagen all day."

The great feeling Peter Bathurst gave him was that he did in some fundamentally mysterious and manly way belong to the world. It did not matter how others looked upon him. Peter Bathurst told him how he should look upon himself. That he was of the First Nations, a warrior, and a man.

But he belonged only to Peter Bathurst's act of belonging. He did not belong beyond what Peter Bathurst allowed. Or outside the web of ideas that Peter Bathurst somehow controlled.

And now he went about town as faithful as a slave to do something because Peter Bathurst had asked him to. He had not sat down to figure out why.

He forgot about his sick old grandmother for the moment. He forgot also about his chronic sore tooth. He drank more wine.

He had found himself drawn into all of this on the way to see his grandmother. He had only been a hanger-on, who after a beer and pickled egg would go and tell his friends how much Peter Bathurst cared for him. And how Peter had talked to him about flying to Washington. Louis liked to tell this story because it was the hallucination of power, and besides, he had never himself been on a plane.

He came up the snowy back street and turned toward the water.

The air was fresher now, and though the snow was still falling, it was not falling steadily. The reserve behind him was silent, the river in front of him was covered in fresh unmarked snow, and drifts were piled up across the river at Shackle's barn.

He turned at the bridge and started toward the reserve again, walking along the snowy bank of the river toward Zeller's, which had a lone car in the parking lot. He felt youthful and heroic, and felt condemned to destroy himself by some kind of heroic action because of his father's agonizing death – a father he had actually loved. He remembered his father's sad face and the tears in his father's eyes the night he died.

And thinking of his father, who had once forced him to eat sour pickles on a bet, Louis might have passed Vicki's maroon car altogether. Except as he was walking by the back door, he heard her sneeze.

He stopped, turned around, and looked at the silent river. Shackle's barn lay in a kind of mid-afternoon twilight. And then the sneeze again. He looked at the car then, smiled, and ran, ran to find Peter Bathurst.

Her grandfather was supposed to call from Anna and Neil's. At two-thirty she decided to telephone them, but the lines were down.

As always she felt there was no one but her.

Sometimes Pumpkin liked to think of Neil and Anna. What great lives they had. And all of those books. When she got older and away on her own, she would have a whole lot of books. She thought of the study she would have, the crystal glasses, the quiet laughter of friends.

She sometimes thought she would like to be like Anna. When she was younger she even practised a slight limp. She would say: "Yes, thank you – no, not at all a trouble." Because Anna had said this to Vicki one afternoon long ago.

There was a graciousness she might imitate, a posture she might try. The idea that had never left her since she had visited them and had walked by the duck pond, and had gone in a punt one day with Anna rowing, was that she would go back there to live when she went to university. And that they wanted her back.

Anna had told her that day about once being coxswain in a rowing club. Pumpkin had put her hands in the water and Anna's face, nose longer than normal, had seemed nonetheless beautiful. And it was clear to her she was in love with Anna, and they would go on trips.

Pumpkin had said self-effacingly that night, after they had come back from a drive in the Volvo, that she would like to live there forever. Anna's black cat, Sebastian, sat under an opened window looking out at the street. A fan whirred and Neil smiled. The smile was artifice and held the terrible dislike of the child, which Pumpkin did not realize at that time.

However, one night last year, coming home from the bar, after drinking most of the evening with some friends, her pants tight about her hips, she had suddenly seen herself as that child. She saw, as clear as a knife wound, Neil's smile, her little Louisa May Alcott book, and she stopped walking. She froze on the street before the bridge because she had remembered Neil's smile. She had remembered holding her Louisa May Alcott book in her hand like leaves of gold, the printed words golden dust on the page.

She was nothing – her whole life was nothing at all. And Neil's smile only betrayed the truth. That moment near the bridge last year, at the moment when she realized this, she was deeply, deeply ashamed. Everything she had ever thought gentle about her father – his huge neck like a boxer's, his powerful wrists – was swallowed alive by Neil's smile. And for the first time, when she realized it all, she felt an affinity for Louis Gatineau, and knew why he did and said the things he did, out of torment and shame.

She sat in front of the mirror in her room on this Easter weekend afternoon. She looked out the window – the snow might stop. And now and then a car would chug by, and she would hope for a signal light – for Neil and Anna to come in.

She had been left behind. She was the one, over the cheap tricks the years played, that had been left out. But still there was a chance. She would not go to Vancouver. She would not bother to approach Neil – she would approach Anna instead.

A thousand times she had decided what she would say, what she would wear when they came, and how she would act. But of course she knew from experience that when she saw Anna all that would go out the window and she would act like a silly teenager.

Her imagination flitted away not to when Anna and Neil came in today and called out to her, but to the coming summer. Next summer she and Anna would be living together. There would be huge flowers, the smell of new paint from back-yard fences. She would be getting ready to go to university – someone, a boy, would call her – Neil would wave.

Then as always in her daydream she was in Anna and Neil's library and up on a footstool: "Oh, I'm just lookin for a volume on Wordsworth," she would say, and Anna would smile in a gust of tenderness. There would be a light on somewhere and the piano would be playing, and then it would be dinnertime.

"Oh, yes, thank you – no, not at all a trouble."

Still her world was different somewhat.

It was as different as a boot in the head.

She did not know when she had discovered her parents to be what they were. Perhaps it was after she came home from her visit to Anna's that summer, and her mother was sitting crosslegged on a broken lawn chair in the heat, her hair dyed and smoking a long cigarette. Pumpkin could tell there had just been a fight and they didn't want to listen to her talk to them about the pond, or the Louisa May Alcott book, or having had sherbet.

Or it may have been on the beach. They were lying on the beach and she looked over, saw the scars on Garth's back and face. Looking up she saw her mother was crying. Or it could have been any other time, any time at all.

She remembered her life in intervals, made longer by endless shrouds of snow. Shrouds upon shrouds. She recalled the apartment building they had lived in before they moved back to her grandfather's farm, a woman named Gretta Bartibog who would come and see her and ask about Reggie. Diane Bartibog, who once took her to Zeller's where they drank Coke from the fountain, and Diane whispered, "I am your first cousin," and bought her a bag of chips.

A bald man who gave her a chocolate and always

smelled like he'd just sat in a barber chair even though he was bald. He said he was old Tom's brother, Nathanial.

Her dog, Folly, that Reggie had bought for her sixth birthday that Vicki took away from her and put in the barn. Years passed. They were always fighting about Verriker and how much money he could spare for them. Fighting and fighting, and she was on her bed listening to them. And sometimes to stop them fighting she would walk into their bedroom, and she would dance.

She would begin to laugh and dance, so they would stop, and stop and stop!

Her mother on those red-leafed October afternoons would cosy up to Verriker on the phone. Verriker's wife, some well-groomed college woman from Medford, would whisper: "It's that terrible Canadian woman again, Brian."

"I'm Canadian, too – remember that," Verriker would say. Garth once told Verriker to change his phone number so Vicki wouldn't be able to bother him. But Verriker couldn't. Because of not being on the ice in the world championship so long ago. He couldn't. And Vicki knew how to measure his guilt. All of this happened, in flicks and reels of sadness on some faraway screen that Pumpkin thought of today.

One night she saw them in the living room. Vicki was standing over her father, who was sitting in a chair staring at nothing. It was as if the marriage had ended at the moment. This was after the man, Professor Wheem, published one of his hockey articles.

More years passed. Down the long stretch between the sheds on old Tom's property, with rabbit wire hanging on the cold, cold nights. Snow fell and fell.

For a while after Vicki came back from university they went to a small church with a lay preacher who interpreted the Bible. He said 6,987 people would be saved, and they were three of them. But sometimes he wouldn't be happy with them. He would say only 6,984 people were going to be saved. They were all like little children, Pumpkin and Vicki and Garth, until Pumpkin outgrew them. For the last seven years she tried to take care of them.

But now Pumpkin was going to ask Anna if she could go and live with her. Her speech would have to be civil and correct and gracious. It would drip off her tongue like chocolate, because she felt her life depended on it. She would not speak ill of Garth or Vicki. She would not tell on them. Ever. Ever. Ever.

Because she loved them so, so much.

"Oh, yes, thank you – no, not at all a trouble."

Tracy McCaustere understood that in almost every case justice for her native client depended today on her promotion in the courtroom of the knowledge that things for him were formerly uncivil or unjust. Truth for her clients was always determined by her this way. In the world truth could be determined.

Now Peter, lumbering and slow, had come to her again to view the documents she had collected that would be used in the discovery against him.

He felt that no one accusing him at this moment gave a damn for the money he'd taken, they only wanted to ruin him. But his lawyer told him there was no way she could stop the process now, and so he would have to be humiliated. Though still in his forties, he looked old and tired, like a man who has just found out he's been betrayed by someone and that that someone was himself.

He thought of the rabbit in the snow again. It was strange – so long ago. It was in 1961. They had been trapping rabbits far beyond the Shackle property that day. He and little Gregory Pie. They came to a river and his cousin Gregory went out onto the ice, holding a stick. But Gregory went through the ice. Peter reached his cousin and hauled him out. Then they had a long way to walk – seven or eight miles, a long way – and he had no matches to start a fire.

Tracy had already received certain papers from the police and brought them out to show him now. She thought that this, in itself, was a rather remarkable coup, and that he would be as happy as she was with it. Peter watched her as she started handing him documents and receipts that would be used against him and his little company of Commix.

He put his glasses on, which made him look grandfatherly, and as she handed him a paper he looked at it, clearing his throat and moving his head up and down, which showed the wrinkles on his neck. As he scanned the page, he had a look on his face that suggested he was searching for a flaw, and once he found it he would tell her what it was. And for the moment this was what she was willing to pretend they were going to find.

The air was deadly quiet in this room now.

There was also Tracy's quiet, serene, and implacable sense of timing as she handed him one dossier and then another.

He saw his own handwritten and blotted numbers coming to light, all of them self-incriminating.

"Did you know that my cousin Gregory froze to death?" he asked suddenly.

"Oh, no – when?" Tracy said, startled, as a person will who expects the tragedy of someone else's life to enliven hers.

"Oh, long time – in the winter a long time ago," Peter said.

"Oh," Tracy said, but she sounded just slightly disappointed. He nodded because he had nothing much else to tell her. And he went back to the papers.

He never thought things would come to this. That all the laughter and frivolity in a Delta hotel that he had shared with Mickey Dunn would be on a paper somewhere that Diane Bartibog had collected to use against him. And of course all the other incidents too. He did not know what to say. His thick hands trembled. Why would Diane Bartibog do this to him? It had to be because of LeRoy. It was a very strange and mechanical kind of act. A kind of snitching. A kind of act that showed how the new world worked. First they had worked against him and everything he did, to get him to fail, and then they brought his failure to court. And he thought of Diane's skinny legs walking hurriedly and realized that this is how things were. He thought of Reggie, and how her marvellous smile reminded him of her father.

Again, too, he remembered her husband counting the money from the box earlier that afternoon. It had been his ambition that made him think he alone could make everyone rich in the end.

"My cousin," he said. "He tried to make it – I tried to carry him – no one would pick us up or give us a drive – he was only 'ittle." Suddenly he felt tears come to his eyes, as if the years had disappeared and he remembered his cousin's gentle smile. The borrowed suit that Gregory wore in the coffin, the little childlike grimace on his mouth.

Then he proudly lifted his glasses and brushed those tears quickly away. He looked at another paper.

As always there was no time to stop – before – before was the time. And again the hot feeling of his innocence washed over him. Again he felt plagued by memories that Tracy wouldn't have a clue about.

As she handed him one paper he would hand back the paper he had. There were names on these papers of friends and acquaintances. And of all of these people who had once stood beside him, not one would take the chance to help him now.

He took to clearing his throat and being startled at each new sheet.

"Oh, well, this here, you see – you see this here." And he shook his head as if he had just been told a terrible secret about someone else.

And he pointed to an illegible mark of seven thousand dollars for a trip that was invoiced to the band, one snowy Scotch-drinking February weekend two years before, when he had hired an escort-service woman, and had talked to her all night innocently about Indian rights and Oka.

"This here," he said with a scowl. But in his soul was the nauseating agony of suffering because he felt he was innocent, and the painful embarrassment that all of this had come to light. Still, even in the midst of this, he saw his cousin's gentle smile when, to warm him, Peter had put his own coat over him. It was as if his cousin's spirit was very close to him now and wanting to tell him something. Wanting to tell him, in fact, what Mary had told him earlier in the day. To stop. To stop. Now, however, was not the time to stop.

He remembered running after cars trying to flag them down, with the little boy on his back, but the cars kept going, wind and snow blowing up behind them.

And then suddenly he stopped reading. Suddenly his mouth pursed, and he looked as if he'd had enough. As if he knew some information that he couldn't tell her yet. That was it – there was a good deal of hidden information that he as a member of the band refused to tell her. So he simply refused to speak anymore.

And it was this look Tracy pretended to understand and pretended to be dismayed about. She did not know the history behind it. But it was this look she had been expecting for a long time.

"Why can't you tell me, and help clear yourself – why?"

However, he was remembering his cousin, that afternoon in 1961. He remembered his cousin wanting to get home to see his mother. And he realized that not much of what happened today mattered. Again his cousin's spirit seemed very near, and he thought of suicide.

Peter looked at Tracy and blinked. And at the heart of this affair was a curious idea Peter had as he held the papers in his hand. The idea was that for Tracy McCaustere's benefit things must be done that would not reveal the truth.

It was this fabrication that he clung to, as a drowning man to a lump of straw. Diane Bartibog had the pole and each new dossier kept pushing his head under the water.

In reality he knew Tracy had egged him on. Maybe she hadn't meant to. But she also knew she had. She had egged him into many fights with the RCMP over the fishing treaty, just last year. She had wanted to win something not just for him but for herself.

She had told him he should always exercise his rights and, over the years, he had come to believe that he was invincible, and, thinking this, their eyes met and Tracy glanced away. So he said nothing. In a way she had egged him on just as she had done with that pimple-faced boy over his attack on Dexter years ago. Now she was ashamed she had done this. She smiled and told Peter that all would be better soon. But Peter wanted to tell her something else. He wanted to confess something, anything. His little cousin had looked up to him so much – and he had failed him. That was when his real failure had begun.

"My cousin dere was eight years ole – no one would pick us up on da road dat day – eight years ole – I carry him as good as I could do. I tried. I was ten year old. It was getting dark. I was scared, and it was so cold. And he didn't think I was scared, his big cousin, who always protect him. It was getting dark and no car would pick us up. His mother wait for us. I tried – no one would pick up – see. I tried. I tried." Peter suddenly remembered his cousin's tiny body pressed against him, and the faith his cousin had had in him to get them home. Then he looked up at Tracy with the same kind of startled look children sometimes have, and the wind, the wind blew.

"Of course," she smiled. "Of course you tried."

And then he said nothing. He moved his feet and was silent. For perhaps there was nothing more to ever say.

As always, his people had to perform tricks in whatever way was acceptable, or her people would just turn away.

I t was almost an hour later. The snow was still falling
heavily. Diane Bartibog paced and smoked in the
kitchen of her house just south of the bridge.

She stopped pacing a moment, and blew smoke from
her thin childlike mouth. Her eyes were small and brown,
her cheekbones high and somewhat chiselled. Her raven-
black hair with just a touch of white was parted in the
middle. She was thirty-four years old, in control of the
band, and sitting near her was Peter Bathurst. He had
come to her, in the end. At this moment Peter was feeling
desperate enough to offer her anything.

He held his reading glasses in his hand and sat with his
elbows on his knees, looking both proud and ashamed.

What she was asking was who had fired the bullets at
her house. Peter said that he knew, and that if she would
get the investigation into the missing funds called off, he
would bring her the person who had fired the rifle.

She paced and thought, and said nothing.

Peter was sitting in her kitchen. In one day he had

gone from being youthful and energetic to being old and sick.

"I know who it was did it," Peter said.

She wore a cowhide vest with a moon on the back. She worked sixteen hours a day. She chainsmoked, was writing a book on racism, and had poor eyesight. Her glasses were thick and heavy, and her eyes blinked rather comically when she spoke. She had very large flat feet.

When all of them were children Diane had stopped getting drunk every night. She had other things to do. She had to save herself, and by this save her people.

She had gone away and had taken a course offered by the federal government. She then went to university where she researched the Indian Act, the rights of Status and Non-Status women. Then for four years she disappeared and no one heard much about her. She was silently studying the band, the treaties, the river. She travelled, too, to Alberta to meet her father, Reggie, who was stationed there.

And then suddenly she appeared again, a picture of her with the prime minister.

There appeared also an article on the unwritten history of natives written by her for a Toronto magazine.

Then, as she suspected, Peter Bathurst got in touch with her. Then, as she suspected, white people got in touch with her as well.

Tracy McCaustere asked to represent her.

Diane appeared on talk shows with various well-known white celebrities.

And then she came back to the reserve to do her work. In a way like an archangel, half-white, half-Indian, and knowing whom she sided with.

Power was so easy now that she had it; it did not seem that she had ever had to strive to get it.

She was brilliant and tough-minded, but she had fallen in love, with a man who had left his wife for her, and she knew that this had been a terrible mistake.

Perhaps it was her own husband's people who had fired the shot for publicity. She didn't know. But it would be well if Peter could actually prove it was someone else, and give her someone else's name to take to the police.

The dispute between her and Peter had started very simply. Over a plot of land where the casino was to be built.

Her husband had not wanted it built where Peter wanted it built; and since he was her husband, she could not see why she couldn't do this for him. So she had stalled.

Peter could not envision his people ever turning against him, so he'd begun to spend money. Flaunting himself and his power for a while.

She didn't care now if he was innocent or guilty or even how much money he'd spent. From the very moment she gave into her husband, terrible things happened. They met at the band office. There were eleven people from the eight most powerful families. Everything was almost settled. But then Peter had hesitated. No one ever knew why. But she did.

He wanted Diane but not her husband involved because of his feeling of loyalty toward Mary Francis. Now Diane smoked her cigarette and stared out the window while Peter looked at her.

She picked up her coffee and coughed hollowly into her hand.

Her husband was more involved at the band office than she was, wore a doe's ear on his cowboy belt, and believed that he had created all this new-found power for himself, just as the women he took to bed believed. She knew that he had already dipped into a trust fund for the new sewage system.

She supposed he would blame that on Peter.

"Go get whoever it was," she said, "and perhaps somebody can work something out." Although she knew the investigation into missing funds could not be stopped, was out of her hands.

Peter looked at her, and nodded.

And he went back out – into the snow.


Peter's father had come to see Diane before he had left for St. Mary's reserve.

His old hat in his hand, his socks pulled up beyond his boots with some snow sticking to them. He was sick and, at seventy-eight, had a kind of dissociated look and oddness about him. And seeing this, she had tried to comfort him. He had sat at the table and had told her that Peter did not know where he was but that Peter had not fired the shot through the window. And if she blamed Peter he would say he had done it and go to jail forever, and die.

He had come on his own to tell her husband this. She told him that her husband was rarely at the house. and the old man looked sorry. All of this fuss had started over nothing, and nobody would win, he said. Except her husband, LeRoy, with his unnatural smile and twenty-five-thousand-dollar Jeep.

The old man had looked so sad that it had brought out her natural tendency to love, with her thick glasses and huge smile.

She loved this old man, whom she had known since she was two years old, who every year had taken them out to get a Christmas tree. He used to tell her stories about sleeping squirrels and bunnies, and how you could catch them and make them pets. One day she had called his bluff and had told him to catch her a sleeping squirrel. So out he went with her into the snow, looking about. And sure enough a squirrel was sleeping on a branch of a tree very near her house.

He sneaked up to it, while she watched, wide-eyed, and picked it up. He patted it and then kissed it. Then he whispered a secret in its ear before he set it back on the branch.

Only when she got older did she realize that the poor squirrel was dead, frozen stiff, and that the old man had been waiting for her to call his bluff.

He had come to remind her about this story, before he took the bus, to remind her of how little she once was, with her thick glasses and wonderful laughter and wobbly knees; and how they all used to be, before everything, everything about them had changed.

Peter went back out. It was four o'clock. Everything was darkening and rain, mixed with snow, still fell, although far away the storm was blowing off. He thought of one person. Louis Gatineau. He did not want to, but he felt he would have to blame someone and that someone had to be Louis.

He went back toward the mall.

Louis Gatineau was there. The air was drizzly and wet, the snow had turned grey. Little children, one dressed as an Easter Bunny, walked by. They were the children from Mary Francis's party at the church.

It was when he saw Peter that young Louis realized there was something sensational in all of this, and he was going to be a big part of it. And it was a good feeling to be part of it, since everyone said he was angry and rough, while inside he had always been scared. He was also very happy that a person like Peter would look out for him.

His hair was sticking out, his eyes like black beads. He had just finished the quart of Hermit wine and was staggering on the street. Like all people who are drunk enough to stagger, Louis at first tried to control his lack of control, and then decided to play up to it.

Peter said nothing to him yet. His face was grey. His hair in its braids hung down wet against the shoulders of his army jacket. Peter didn't like Louis when he was drinking. He knew how unpredictable he could be. But the idea of blaming him while he was drunk played, flitted in his mind. Yes. That would be easier.

He would persuade Louis that taking the blame was the right thing to do for the band. It would make his name known, in a manly way, to have fired the shot. If he went to court Peter would be there, to take the stand and give as grand a character reference as one would ever want. Louis might do time and he might not – but his name would be known.

He saw Louis staring up at him like a child waiting for instruction. And he began to speak: "Louis, you and I both know who fired that shot at Diane Bartibog." He said this and he winked as if to draw him closer into a relationship. Louis nodded, shivered in his thin dark clothes, and water dripped from his hair.

"Yes, yes," Louis nodded, like a child, "and I found Vicki for you."

"Vicki – Vicki Shackle?" Peter said.

"Of course – I found her for you."

Louis told him where Vicki was. He exaggerated how he had been able to sneak up on the car, and how he had followed the signs to her. Suddenly, the thrust of Peter's ideas changed. Once again, the idea was to get some money back.

And they turned and started down the snow-covered streets. Sadly for Louis, when they came to the parking lot, the car was no longer there.

"It was here a minute ago," Louis said definitely. Now, however, there was nothing but black snow left from underneath the tires, and the same soft drizzle, while the shadows of the day lengthened against the small stone wall on the opposite shore.

"Where would she go?" Louis said.

"I don't know," Peter said. The car tracks ran under them back toward the mall. "But we couldn't have missed her by more than a minute.

Stung by Louis's faith in him, the idea of blaming him faltered. And Peter turned and started back up the hill. Louis followed. Louis's boots were slippery on the slippery snow, and he kept thinking that this search for Vicki must be because of the shot which had been fired at Diane. Although he had not reasoned it out he felt he was getting close to the intrigue surrounding him.

"You best go home, before this trouble comes on you," Peter said suddenly, trying to face him.

But Louis only laughed. He had all his life wanted to show he was brave. And now was his opportunity.

Louis was now thinking that they were trying to blame Peter for something that Vicki had done and therefore they had to get her and take her to the police. Louis could never think of blaming Peter for anything. He thought how terrible it would be to blame Peter. And he looked at Peter's back as they walked, his strong old back, with its broad shoulders, and thought of the man as the kind father he never had.

They went back to Dunn's. Dunn was standing inside the second room, by the poker machines. He was cursing, looking at Vicki's four loonies and her burned-out cigarette. He held her coat draped over his arm.

Dunn was acting as if this was a terrible injustice to Peter, and that he himself was uninvolved.

Louis was now in a position suddenly – within this inner circle – he did not wish to be in. And it was only with more drinking that he felt he would belong.

He looked at Dunn, who had not stopped cursing.

Yet the talk wasn't even about the rifle shot. It was about the big casino, and how it might still work. Peter spoke about his lawyer and how she would solve everything.

*Guaranteed*, he kept saying. *Guaranteed*.

Mickey Dunn spoke about the man from Devon, and said he was sorry he ever trusted him. But soon he would get everything on track again.

Peter nodded, as if something would be done dramatically to clear him in every way possible. Mickey patted Louis on the back and Louis smiled. The light, airy, sensational feeling came back. And Mickey gave them some rum. Mickey always gave rum to people he was in some way casting off.

They sat drinking for over half an hour. All of them knowing something terrible was to happen, and wanting now to correct it. Finally Peter looked at his watch.

"Let's go," he said.

Louis had no idea where. He only knew he was being

compelled to go along and he didn't know why. He began to laugh and felt he couldn't stop.

Peter told him as they went out the door, with the smell of flat, darkened ice in the middle of the grey afternoon, that they would go to see Diane Bartibog – and this is where they started. Outside, the darkness of the evening enveloped them. Far off, the trees were motionless, beaten at now by the sleet and snow. The air was fresh and small pellets of frozen ice rested upon the power lines. In the lane a power truck was pulled over, and a young man was up on the pole trying to free a line. The world looked at once safe and dismal here. Looking at the trees, at the power lines, listening to the chug of the truck engine, there was still time, time enough to stop.

They were all of them still innocent of almost everything. Peter might have to do a month or so in jail. Yet Peter was now taking Louis to Diane Bartibog's. And Louis was happy to be going. Because that's where *he* would figure everything out. Peter had to figure something out by six o'clock.

Louis trod lightly behind, his hands thrust into the pockets of his worn jeans, staggering and falling, thinking that what must be must be.

At four o'clock Vicki was sitting in the car looking at her poems, smoking a cigarette.

She drove back across town and just on the outskirts of the reserve stopped suddenly to make a phone call to see how Garth was. But the lines were down. Sleet had gathered on the wires. Vicki walked back to the car. If she had not stopped to go to that phone booth, every event that had ever taken place in her life might have culminated in a different way.

∾

Anna was sitting in a small darkened room the following July when she heard this. It was at the back of the tavern in Brickton – just a little place east of Taylorville. A tavern in Brickton made of brick, and one hot airless room with five windows opened to the street and a dense budworm-sprayed wood. Far off was the mill, and the smell of sterile metal in the heat, and beyond that a church with its lonely crucifix.

She had driven up from the university and its blistering new administrative building, called Dexter Hall, which had just opened to a fanfare of wine and cheese and the broadest display of toasts for a man's genius in a place where it never mattered from one day to the next what was believed to be true.

She had come up to collect a few things from Sergeant John Delano, and from her Aunt Caroline.

Pumpkin had brought the horses around, Sergeant Delano said. Sergeant Delano was the man assigned in early 1993 to an outside investigation into the missing funds, then into the gunshot, and subsequently into the war between the two factions on the reserve.

*So Pumpkin had brought the horses in.*

By then it was after four; it was almost dark. The evening had turned to rain and flashes of lightning. In a large room above the stalls, Pumpkin had her money hidden in an oat barrel. It was a quiet room above the stalls, with a few tack chests sitting kitty corner, and a few pictures on the walls. Tracy McCaustere's riding helmet and breeches lay on an English saddle in a closet.

Pumpkin had moved her father into the back room of the house, whether for safety or some other reason, no one knew.

He asked for Vicki, and where Neil and Anna were. Then he had insisted he get dressed, as if he too knew something was about to happen.

She brought the mare and colt into the barn, their backs covered in sleet, and took the coal-black stud from the paddock. She put a blanket over the colt. She whistled in her great large rubber boots.

The barn again was filled with the clopping of hooves and the smell of horse and the feel of wind under the great horses legs as sleet blew in through the doors.

The sky was driven with sleet. In this sleet on every corner of the reserve was the rumour that they had found out who had fired the shot though Diane Bartibog's house that had wounded the little girl. It spread out, like a spill in water, that it was Vicki Shackle.

Sergeant Delano had not been in town to stop the rumour. He had been called to an accident. There he met a Professor Wheem, who had tried to run through the snow. Old Tom Shackle was holding him down because of the cliff fifteen feet away, which Professor Wheem seemed oblivious to.

"He's a bit upset," old Tom was saying. His face had been scratched by Wheem, and three old men had come out of the battered bus to try to calm the professor down.

The Indian man, Bruce Bathurst, was helping Tom by holding Wheem's long legs.

This was just after dark. Sleet was falling through the grey trees. Old Tom was exhausted and would have a heart attack a month later.

It was at this time that Pumpkin was bringing the stud from the paddock, its falling mane like a raven's feathers and its black eyes with red pellets on the side. Its feet needing to be shod, its hooves cracked in the sleet which

188

made such a magnificent animal look, when one noticed his feet, sorrowful.

Vicki had already gone to the phone and had come back. When she reopened the door to her LeMans, it creaked and the wind caught it.

Sergeant John Delano had not advanced as much as he had hoped, a fact that was reinforced by his smart eyes, his solid cheekbones, by the idea that his own death would be viewed by him, and his squabbling ex-wives, as not so important. His hair was thin and grey and he had a smart toothbrush moustache. He had not liked Mr. Dunn.

It was said he had never particularly liked women. His divorces came because of his dislike of women probably – though not his dislike of his children. His children sadly were what his wives held over him now. Like some out-of-favour centurion of a bygone age, he had been placed in the hinterland of the province.

He had known Vicki.

He pushed an envelope toward Anna and smiled sadly. It was what he had collected about the debts incurred by Vicki and Garth over eight years.

In this envelope was the story of Vicki's university days. All of the evidence on her and Wheem horribly explicit. How Garth sold his only possession. A racehorse.

The racehorse snapped a bone and the new owner, Mr. Dunn, accused Garth of selling him a bad horse.

To compensate for this Garth swept up at Mickey's bar – a place he and Vicki had once owned.

When one Friday Garth came to collect his paycheque Mickey Dunn handed a slip to him. "You already owe me four thousand dollars," Mickey said. In the envelope were the receipts Garth had kept in trying to pay this mounting debt off. Each week he got an advance in money and would then have to send it to Vicki. In ten months he fell fourteen thousand in debt.

After she came home from university she spent the rest of her life trying to get the money back for him.

If he hadn't played that hockey game, if he had not gone over the boards, if he had not thought of grabbing the puck in his skate – IF.

Delano took the envelope and held it and looked back over his shoulder and then looked at Anna, his eyes averted just slightly.

Anna cleared her throat as if some dust had caught in it. Her face was too white.

A few Indian men were drinking silently in the corners of the tavern. A gust of wind came in.

Anna had tears in her eyes. Garth had always called her "sad Anna" and he loved to hear her stories about university days, and hallowed hallways in places like Ridley School.

Her tiny body, her lameness, always made her seem gentle to him, special somehow.

Sometimes he made an attempt to say important things, but then he would smile as if the world had beaten him down. If Neil was there he would put his head down or grin.

She had told him once after his injury that, like Jacob in the Bible, he was made lame for one great purpose, after he had wrestled with an angel of God.

"I wrestle with an angel of God every night," he said. "I wrestle with Vicki."

∾

In the cool grey dark, Pumpkin climbed the stairs at four-thirty to her father's room.

Garth was sitting up, bent over trying to dress himself. His huge shoulders were white and bony, puck marks all over his stomach and chest. Flat ones, round ones, and ones on the edge. In the dark he looked like an apparition who had always been there, waiting for the door to open and for outsiders to come and view him. You saw his hands first and then his stomach, white and still taut, his yellowed ribcage, permanently altered, his shoulders sloping more to the right than the left. His huge, muscled back bent forward, as if centuries ago he was some rower on a slave ship.

"Where is she?" he asked, whispered into the hard darkening room. "She cannot pay any money for a casino that isn't even built. I want to phone the police," he said. "But I can't get anything on the phone – bring the shotgun –"

The room was cool, and Garth reached for his cane. He

looked at Pumpkin but said nothing. She had been wearing perfume and tight clothes now for as long as he remembered, but it was as if he just now realized what it all was for.

"Help me up," he said finally. "Where's Neil and Anna – have they come?"

"Not yet," Pumpkin said. "They're either in an accident or they're not coming."

∾

The envelope John Delano handed Anna contained much that was supposedly hidden from everyone. After Vicki came home from university, they tried religion. They tried Reverend Matheson and his Lumberman's Crusade. They tried tent meetings. They wore "Keep the Faith" T-shirts; they got into selling Amway, went to meetings across the province.

Once they went to Boston.

They met Verriker at a restaurant downtown. It was the last year of his NHL career. They went to the Garden. Garth had wanted to see the great Denis Savard play, and Chicago was in town.

Pumpkin did not know who Denis Savard was – nor that her own father would have been in his league.

It was Boston; it was where Garth should have been.

Suddenly eighteen years of anger at what had happened to her husband came over Vicki. And crying, she began to accuse Verriker of never doing enough for them – of not being on the ice, of Garth taking the hit, and trading places with him.

"Look at him," she said. "Take a look –" It was the most hopeless, and the proudest, statement about her husband she had ever managed to make.

Verriker, tears in his eyes, said, "If you need anything – anything – anything!" He smiled at Pumpkin: "Eat your cake, darlin, eat your cake."

Garth sat there, as if he, being the subject matter, was no longer present in the room. In his hand he held Denis Savard's autograph.

∽

The mid-afternoon heat was stifling. It bore down on the shelterless streets of Brickton and the foundry, the plywood mill, the paper mill far away, and wrestled against the certain vacant dress shops that stood with empty longing, their doorways opened.

Anna asked Sergeant Delano: "Did they want us to take Penny?"

"Vicki wanted you and Neil to take her from the time she was two years old, but could not bring herself to ask, thinking she would be looked upon as a bad mother –"

"But it would have been the kindest act for us all," Anna said, quietly. In tragedy naivety plays the greatest role.

John Delano told Anna things she did not know. In 1989 Garth fell in love, with Jenna Wheem. They were going to go away.

Vicki implored Jenna on her knees in St. Brenden's. It seemed Vicki had nothing left.

A plain short woman with a freckled face looking at a woman on her knees, a gambling addict, whose beauty could turn the world on its side.

And Jenna smiled kindly. "I'll not have a sister on her knees to me," she whispered, and brought her up.

A car went by and cast a shadow on the table where they sat.

∾

And Louis and Peter continued walking toward the reserve. Peter began the process of talking to Louis about his confession. He would ask him to do this for him. If he did, Louis would never have to worry any more. This was what he was trying to say, while Louis walked behind him. Feeling it was his only hope, and that he could not stop now, Peter turned to speak. Louis abruptly stopped walking, and smiled up at him.

Yet as Peter turned he noticed Vicki's car sitting above them, twenty feet away. And Vicki staring at them both like a feral cat caught in a corner.

"There she is," Peter whispered.

∾

It was now eight years since Dexter's death. He was now more socially accepted than he had been when he was alive. Though still obscure, his books had all been re-printed, and his house had become an immaculate kind of tourist shrine, became a wayward pilgrimage for certain young people fraught with a kind of angst that Dexter never had.

He had been picked up on the street by John Delano for drunkenness many times. Some nights Delano would take him to his own trailer, and they would talk.

Sergeant Delano, with his reddish hands and his dark eyes, wanted to learn. He had spent his entire life wanting to know. And he respected this man. But Emile told him nothing he did not already know, and Emile was doomed.

Now Anna told Sergeant Delano Emile was talked about in restaurants in Toronto, and in writing confer-ences at Blessed Falls, Ontario.

It was, Anna smiled, not that they ruined him, or tried for his death, but that the system did. Yes, it was the system.

Anna went later that afternoon to visit Dexter's mother. It had been seven years.

Anna viewed the place again – the garden, the narrow walkway out to a small greenhouse, and beyond, those dark pools of water that he wrote about. She carried the envelope Sergeant Delano had given her.

Her aunt seemed something of an elder stateswoman. She had become part of the fabric of Dexter's writing life.

It no longer mattered what was true or not true about him, how she had wanted him to be a nice boy; that at one time she could not play bridge with her neighbours because of the swearing in his books.

Everything had changed about who he was, and that was to everyone's benefit now. Her aunt didn't like Mr. Delano saying he was a friend of his, for he was never about when Emile was "at his best." And her aunt now believed that those people in Taylorville who had never glanced in his direction had been his friends, while Sergeant Delano, who had picked him up on the street for safety's sake, had just used him. "People like John Delano who've always had a terrible reputation here," she smiled. "Married three times, you know."

She asked about Neil; Anna stared off into the distant trees. It was a hot and wonderful summer afternoon, although with just a hint of sombre dark clouds on the horizon.

She shook her aunt's worn hand and turned once to look at the upstairs window. There was something cold in Mrs. Dexter's look, something of the vindicated village tyrant.

Then Anna drove just a little way out of town. Beyond the mill, beyond the wiener-and-chip stand in the hot air, beyond the self-absorbed trees was a small park where she stopped. She sat on the park bench and waited for evening to come.

She stared at the envelope. How Vicki had hated her too. And who could blame her now?

She often remembered the painters, the frozen galleries with their colour-blind pictures of her Maritime heritage that she and Neil would inspect in their younger years.

She remembered the false praise that came to everyone's lips after Wheem's play about good feminist men. She remembered the terrible waste of time.

Even Wheem's self-interest had a blinding sadness, and made her feel love for him in the fruitless agony of small poetry readings in pitiless snowstorms and in those same snowstorms the smell of futility in half-dark, entirely empty university offices.

But all that was long ago. Today she wore a light summer skirt and carried a small change purse. The brace on her leg silver in the sun.

Neil was now president of the university and had an office in Dexter Hall. That was why he could not make it home that Holy Thursday. A reception honouring that appointment was held that very afternoon. Nor did Anna know how much he had politicked for it.

It was going now. Her periods were becoming irregular, her face was wan and tidy, her small body was compact and still, her breasts like small oranges, but there was such a sadness about her. Everyone had noticed this for a long while now.

The great stillness that is sadness came over her on the green, and down along the duck pond, where she sat on the stone bench remembering Penny, and where she now walked alone.

It was not mysterious. It was rather ordinary. She had

lost her youth. She had lost her hope. And she had taken a young student under her wing. Perhaps she was self-interested. But if so, it may have been the only self-interest she had ever shown.

She bought the girl things, helped her move into a fresh, roomy apartment with a large window.

She loved the girl as much as anyone had. The girl was pregnant and she bought her things.

Anna planned to adopt the child. But the young woman was frightened and young and took the other option – the increasingly more civilized one; the one recommended. She did not tell Anna for many weeks after.

The young woman wondered if she would have to leave the apartment, or pay some money back. Of course not. For Anna loved her and could not blame her.

It was in the evening seven months later when she found out. It was supposed to be the child's due date. Anna and Neil were sitting at home by themselves. Neil only confessed because the young woman had been so distraught at the moment and she had telephoned him, to blame him. Neil couldn't stand blame. He spoke to Anna later about how alive the young woman had been. She had come to his class, and for the first time in years, his sense of truth in poetry was reinvigorated. Did Anna understand how important this was for him? Her memorable honour's thesis on Browning's assertion that "the misapprehensiveness of his age is exactly what a poet is sent to remedy." How refreshing this was for him. And then of course her particularly brilliant paper on "Fra

Lippo Lippi." He asked Anna if she would like to see a copy of it.

Anna had been holding some adoption papers in her hand.

Neil was always so proper now, the moons of his fingernails were so immaculate. He nervously looked about as he spoke. The den was darkened, ruefully decorated. A small picture of Pumpkin and Anna at the beach sat on the piano. The cello case was zipped shut.

She stood. And the fact was that when Anna stood up too quickly she would always tumble sideways into a wall; which is what she did.

"Oh," she said. "Clumsy."

She still had the adoption papers in her hand. She looked at them. "How stupid of me," she said, but it didn't seem to be about the papers.

Her small eyes blinked as if she were focusing on something far away. She smoothed her skirt and immediately decided she had to go to the window. That seemed imperative. Far up the hill the university sat dead in the heat.

"I'm so sorry," she said, because her lame leg began to tremble.

Betrayal seemed very common now. She sat on the bench in the small park, looking at the endless haze. In the end, though, Vicki did not betray anyone any more.

∽

Peter went toward Vicki, and said he must see Garth. That they must phone Verriker. She must understand that so much went into the plans for the casino, and that it did not mean it was over. The casino would still be built or his name wasn't Peter Bathurst. Yet at this moment his voice sounded far away – not his own.

Vicki got out of the car to speak to them. It was twenty minutes to five in the afternoon.

"Come on, " Peter said, while Louis stood beside him. "You owe us this money. I don't want it – but if I don't have it by six tonight," Peter said, "you'll end up in jail –"

Louis did not know what this was about but it seemed to be appropriate to him at the moment. And so he tried to look both angry and tough, and spoke out loud, and laughed.

Vicki nodded and went back to the car to get her purse. Still, at this moment, everything was normal. There was only one thing. She decided from the time she left Peter until she got into the car that none of them were ever going to bother Garth again. And she started the car, took a breath and a lingering drink of gin and smiled.

She missed them in her attempt to run them down and went across the street and hit a culvert. Louis yelled, gave something of a war yelp. Getting out of the car she swung at the air with her purse and started to run.

"One must remember," John Delano had said, "that this was the most terrible act of defiance she had ever mustered for the benefit of someone she had always loved.

And," he continued, "Louis himself felt he too had to show someone, anyone, defiance."

Louis didn't want to do anything really. But he was compelled to act, because he had joined in something that was already crumbling about him, like an empire folding under his feet. Louis's father had always told him only one thing: "When a man insults you, don't forgive it, don't forget it."

And with this was the idea that he must please everyone who now expected something from him. Louis's idea was that Vicki had fired the shot and was now trying to escape justice. In fact if anyone had told Louis it was about money, he would not have believed them.

"I'll go get her," he said, and he became excited by his own voice.

Peter put his large hand on Louis's neck and held him back. "Not now," he said. "We have to figure this out."

∾

Mickey was lying down. He was having his afternoon nap on the dark worn couch in the office when they came back in.

He said there was nothing he could do for them now. They were both soaking wet, and Louis Gatineau had an unpleasant odour of wine. He was soaking wet, having fallen many times.

By four o'clock on Holy Thursday, Mickey felt he had cleared himself of any obligation to Peter Bathurst, so he would not now go to Vicki's house with them. Peter did not want to go to the Shackle house alone. As strange as it might seem to those who would not know, he was always hesitant to go onto a white man's property alone.

Yet over the last three days Mickey Dunn had realized that Peter Bathurst was no longer in control of anyone, had no money, nor influence with his people. It didn't matter if Peter was innocent or guilty. Mickey never once thought of this. A month or so ago Mickey had approached the very people who had ousted Peter. That is, since the election, Mickey was in constant contact with Diane Bartibog's husband. Today Diane Bartibog's husband had counted out twenty thousand in seed money for the new project, and he would donate his land as well.

Mickey was surprised that Peter hadn't heard. The Devon man would be contacted again, because he had links to the Department of Indian Affairs. But it had to be done *properly* this time. It was as if, now that they were rid of Peter, all of this *would* happen. And as if it was Peter's fault alone that it hadn't happened before.

How strange and sad it was that Peter was still running to Vicki's house for money she didn't have.

Peter looked at him. He smelled the bar, saw the leather couch with Mickey's indentation still on it, and felt lost. Except for one thing. He realized he could not, no matter what, give Louis up to them. He would go to jail first.

*Don't leave the church – stay here – it will be worse if you go out.*

It was now after five in the evening, and they were out on the street again.

Peter knew that his father would not be phoning him with news about the money. Worse, he understood business from Mickey Dunn's point of view. He understood others had taken his place. And he remembered that the same thing had happened to an old chief ten years before, and how he had always applauded it, for it had given him his first taste of power.

Louis looked up at him, as if for some instruction, and Peter's heart ached for the boy.

*Don't get him into this*, a voice whispered, almost at the same instant as he heard another voice, his own, speaking.

"Go get her; she'll phone Verriker for us. I've been betrayed by white men for the last time."

He had to prove to everyone that he could see things through himself. Now was not the time to stop. Before – even an hour ago – that was the time. When he was sitting in Diane Bartibog's kitchen was the time. Now was the time to do something else, something more.

"I can't go onto their land – but you can," Peter heard himself say. "You can. You know them – you do this for me!"

"Their land – it's all our land," Louis shouted. "It's always been all our land!" And, at least in a certain way, he was right.

The wind, the sleet, the howling air, had suddenly become still.

All of this was almost exactly as Emile Dexter had written ten years before.

Vicki climbed the stairs, falling and rolling back down and climbing them again. She was half-drunk and ranting and raving about them wanting to phone Verriker.

"Goddamn Verriker," she kept shouting. "They are not going to touch Verriker."

And Garth started down from his room with a small .410 shotgun. He broke it, looking for a shell. As far as he was concerned now, although far away in Boston this would not be known, he was protecting Verriker from scoundrels.

"Who is it, Dunn and Bathurst, where are they?" he said trying to reach for a box of shells. He had no idea he was carrying a gun until that moment, and he seemed to have said this just to scare Vicki, who had scared him when she had clambered up the stairs.

"Let's go find them," Vicki said, pausing to light a cigarette and then clearing her throat. For her, too, now was not the time to stop. She felt exactly as she did when she gambled. It was never the time to stop, because even when she was losing, even then, she still felt she had power and control. The sky was clearing and stars were peeping through. In fact if you looked quickly it reminded you of the picture on the back of Diane Bartibog's vest.

Ten minutes passed. It took time for Louis and Peter to get across the bridge and move up the snowy dark bank at the far side of the barn.

"Did she fire the shot?" Louis asked, "I want to know. Maybe I'll burn her barn. Show her whose property she's on." He went to the back of the barn and found the jug of diesel gas.

There was a light on in the porch at the back of the barn, and the inside arena lights were now on. Upstairs he could see the dim glow from the office. He walked with purpose. He walked with purpose partially because of a fight he had had the night before, and partially because he wanted to show Pumpkin how well he could walk. And partially because he needed to be tough, because they told him his father had died from drinking Lysol. Because he knew somewhere that people would hear what was about to happen, and he wanted to outdo everyone who had ever thought little of him.

He laughed, his chin soaking with rainwater: "You're limping," he said to Peter Bathurst.

Louis had been talking exceptionally erratic for ten minutes and Peter Bathurst was drawing farther back. He had never, from the time he was a child, gone onto any white man's land unless invited.

Peter heard himself shouting, telling Louis to go home.

Louis laughed as if to question this, his eyes dark and blazing, and then he began to bang on the side of the barn. If you want to belong, his eyes seemed to say, this is what it comes to.

"This is our land – come out, come out, wherever you are," he shouted in a heavy drunken voice, his hair soaking. His voice trailed off in the wind. Upstairs in the barn Pumpkin took her money from the oat barrel and put it in her pocket. She thought Louis must have come for more money for the train, and she was willing to give him twenty more dollars. She heard him shouting downstairs, telling her to get out.

Upstairs in the house, two hundred yards away, the lights had been turned out. The television wires rattled against the shingles, and an old board slapped.

" 'I wish that I could fight like my brother in the army,' " Garth sang. He turned and smiled at his wife, who had known more men than he had women. He bolted the gun and looked out the window. His back was lacerated with a skate mark. He began to laugh. She was breathing against his back, her nose so close to his skin it was tickling him. She had been following him for five minutes as if she were stuck to him. She said she was afraid she was going to wet her pants. And he realized that she had always been frightened, and he was sorry for that now. She had always been frightened of everything, and of every one of them.

" 'I don't know where he's stationed – be it Cork, or in Killarney.' "

She touched the tattoo on his arm of the woman named Margaret he had known in Vancouver, when he thought they were done with one another. She didn't mind this any more. How he had suffered. He had been an errand boy for Dunn for seven years, to pay for a university career where men effectively spit in his face.

Yet a parasite can take only so much blood before his victim is willing to turn and fight to the end.

The last person Garth wanted to hurt was Peter Bathurst, who had never done him wrong and who had never even been on his land before today.

Then came the phoney war, which lasted for about ten minutes. No one knew at all what happened. Except that Vicki went to the fridge and got a chocolate bar. Garth was gritting his teeth and blood was coming slowly from his mouth. Then they all started yelling and shouting about money – who owed whom money.

Then came Garth's first shot from the upstairs window.

Then the phoney war was over.

The day was black now. Evening would shoulder the blame. Then from inside the barn they saw a bit of smoke, not much.

"Christ, they set the barn on fire," Vicki said. Both of them stared out the window of a dark forlorn house in the middle of nowhere, like two schoolchildren.

Garth said he needed to go and help Pumpkin. They needed to get the horses out.

Peter Bathurst knew he could not stop anything now. Before – before was the time to stop. When he was with Mary Francis was the time. When he was with Mickey Dunn, when he had bothered Vicki, that was the time.

Now – now it was different. Now he wanted to stop, but Louis couldn't. Now too his innocence or guilt didn't seem to matter.

Louis said it was their barn and their land, and suddenly acted as if this was what the fight must be about. Peter tried to get him to come with him. For ten minutes he tried to get him from the barn.

But Louis could not leave now. There was nowhere for him to go. He was now on the edge of a cliff where to prove himself meant he had to fly.

Peter could not fly. "I'm gonna get water and put these goddamn fires out," he said in Micmac, and desperately he ran from the barn.

Vicki was helping Garth, who was hobbling back and forth on a cane with a shotgun in his hand. They kept bumping into things and missing turns along the halls because it was so dark. The old house creaked like it had long held a ghost.

"Some spooky with the lights out," Vicki whispered as she looked out the window.

She saw Peter Bathurst, and she thought he was coming to kill them.

They started having a discourse on the idea of firing a gun. How much did it kick, would it hurt her shoulder? What would the range be? And Garth was trying to answer these questions. Suddenly it was as if she were an expert on shells and velocity and kick and range.

You see, though Louis was burning down the barn in

revenge for a gunshot he believed Vicki had fired, Vicki had never fired a gun in her life.

"Here," Garth said when they got to the porch, and he handed her a snow shovel.

"What do I do?"

"Take this shovel and beat someone over the head until they stop breathing."

"I'm never paying another cent!" Vicki shouted into the howling wind. "We both will be dead before we do." And for the first time in her life, she sounded free.

Pumpkin had heard Louis and Peter arguing. Then there was silence. She went to the top of the stairs timidly and looked down. Louis was piling hay up in the back of the indoor arena. Four horses were staring cautiously at him as if they wondered what he was doing.

"Louis – you put those matches away – we already have a fire going – here," Pumpkin shouted, her heart racing, trying to remain calm. "I already can't see for smoke."

"No, no –" Louis said. "Vicki tried to kill Diane Bartibog. That's what I told you."

"She did not do any such thing –"

"Ask Peter –" Louis said. "Your dad is a thief – this is our land – it always has been – he wasn't even a good hockey player."

"What do you mean he wasn't a good hockey player? He was a great hockey player – a wonderful slapshooter, so hand those matches over to me."

The arena lights shone faintly through the smoke,

making shadows here and there, and a few birds fluttered on the crossbeams, watching him.

He tried to look even more serious than lighting a fire would make someone look. He walked about the hay dabbing it with a bit of diesel, and then he lit a cigarette. It was as if in his action he was saying: *You see how you misjudged me – look at how I am now – pretty scary, eh? – you thought you could laugh at me – keep me in the Volkswagen in the dump, sleeping with the mice – give me smallpox. But look at me now.*

"You have to stop," Pumpkin was roaring. "You have to stop."

By now the barn was burning, and Peter came back to the boarded horses to try to get them out. He could not find the light switch here. And again he saw his cousin's smile and became afraid. He let loose as many horses as he could find, but two of them just came back into the barn. He began to slap them, trying his best to get them to move.

Finally there was nothing more that he could do except try to get the police. And he decided that was what he had to do. And he ran across the bridge.

He went back to his house, and sat there with the loaded 30.30 long-barrel Marlin on the bed and a cellular phone in his hand, trying to contact people to get him out of a terrible mess. Then, throwing the phone down, he turned in agony and went back to the bar, to get Mickey, to help him at the barn.

Mickey was sitting stiffly in his leather chair, his feet in loafers on the flat, worn floor. He listened to Peter in the darkness, the trophies of stuffed animals over his head.

"I didn't do this," Mickey said, as Peter spoke. "I didn't do any of this. It was you. I don't give a damn about Vicki Shackle, I always treated her fair."

"I don't give a Christ who treated her fair. I don't give a Christ about you," Peter said. "I don't care about that. It's the barn, it's Louis – it's going to burn! I'm going back to get the rest of the horses out – and if you were any kind of man, you'd come and help me." But Mickey said nothing, seemed too paralyzed to move.

Louis did not know where Peter was. He thought Peter was with him in the terrible duty he had to perform. He hadn't even remembered Peter's blows. Nor did he remember that he had thrown Peter down and had realized that he was younger and more powerful than the older man.

And now he was alone in his duty. His duty to talk, to shout, to take back the land because the salmon pools were theirs.

He kept lighting fires and Pumpkin kept yelling at him. Picking up a pitchfork she started down the stairs.

"Christ, I'm going to have to kill him," she thought. All day she had been waiting for Anna, whom she looked upon as something of an angel, a saviour for her, who had been without a saviour since she was three years old.

And now quite suddenly, because of events over which she had no control, she was doing something she never imagined she would ever do.

Louis did not know why he was lighting all of these fires. He kept throwing burning hay and paper in the air. If anyone had told him that morning when he woke up with his gumboots still on and his workshirt opened, lying on his cot – if anyone had told him that by six-thirty at night he would not be on the train going to visit his grand-mother, but he would be walking about Shackle's barn lighting it on fire, he would have called them insane.

And yet now it was perfectly normal that he was doing this. In fact, it was the only thing a sane man would do. It was not him working for him, but he who had crossed the Rubicon to do things for his people. Except most of his people would understand nothing of it.

There were hideous shouts now about the colt, which had been blanketed. That that blanket had begun to smoulder. The old mare refused to leave the barn, and the colt had run to the back of the barn and stood sideways as if trying to hide.

The great stallion was trapped in its box-stall and moved hopelessly about, and somewhere through the smoke someone was yelling.

At one point Louis passed Garth, as weak as a ghost, trying to lead the Arabian outside.

Everywhere smoke funnelled. And Louis was now thinking: "Well, they are getting the horses out – that's good – because I'm burning down their entire barn."

And thinking this he yelled it out: "You'd better get the horses out because I'm burning the barn – get back for Vicki's killing spree –"

At this point Peter was at the other side of the barn wrestling with Tracy McCaustere's morgan. It was a horse, brown with a white star and two white hooves, that he did not like, ever since it had nipped at him when he had helped her feed it once.

Not knowing what to do, and feeling that he had to do something, unable to find Louis, at that part of the barn near the pile of manure, where no one else was, he simply held the horse's halter and shouted for help. That the horse tossed back its head and broke Peter's hand was something that Peter did not even know.

When Louis's boot caught on fire he wiggled it off and felt the exuberance a man might feel who, when touched by our Lord Jesus, handles a copperhead rattlesnake.

He looked about. Was there anything else he might be able to burn. Sawdust chips, tack, saddles, anything at all.

The great window in the office burst with heat and there was a screech somewhere. He stopped and looked about. His side was bleeding, because Pumpkin had just stabbed him with the pitchfork and called him a maniac and it was he who had screeched.

"What, what, what?" he said. Ten minutes had passed since he had seen Garth with the Arabian.

Now everything was ablaze. And you could smell and hear a terrible thing, burning flesh.

"You don't understand," he said to Pumpkin. "You have to get out of here." And he carried her to the side door of the arena and threw her down. Pumpkin landed on her rump in the snow. Her immediate thought was that it was so clear outside. There were stars, so far away, and nothing here mattered very much at all. She had been thrown down ten yards from Peter and didn't even see him.

She stood and went around to the front of the barn.

She couldn't see anyone. She looked for Anna. She had been waiting for Anna since seven o'clock in the morning.

All of a sudden the idea that Anna wasn't coming – that she would never be able to live with her – filled her and she started to run.

She went to the house. She did not know at this moment that Garth and Vicki were in the barn, and she wanted to get them. But there was no one in their room. Only a small plate with half a morphine tablet and a Crunchie chocolate bar.

She turned and ran back down the stairs and across the front pasture.

On the side of the barn opposite Peter Bathurst, Garth had become trapped between the great stud and the terrible wall and was trying to throw a burlap blanket over the stud's head, while Vicki was running back and forth outside the door yelling at him to come out. Pumpkin hadn't known this was going on and she tramped through the high snow without even seeing her mother.

The barn was a furnace leafed with fires and reminded

Pumpkin of the gold room at Le Chateau where they had gone for sherbet. She turned as quick as a cat and ran to her father's aid, opening the stall door and trying to get up on the stud's back. She fell sideways, was trapped herself, and struggled to get up on it again, but felt one of the horrible hooves coming down on her.

"Hell out of here – go away – Pumpkin – VIC – come in and GET your little girl."

Pumpkin rose gallantly to get the panic-stricken horse by the mane, was flung high, broke her arm, and fell under the horrified horse's hooves.

Outside a crowd had gathered. Men were busy trying to get the horses out. The Arabian had made it, but the blanketed colt and the mare had not. On the far side Peter had got some of the boarders out, but he could hear the terrible whinny of others.

Vicki was roaring at people to do something to help her family, rushing in and out of the barn until her hair caught fire, and she was forced to the ground by a tackle from Hector Wheem.

Hector Wheem then walked back and forth, holding the dog, Folly, who wanted to run into the barn after Pumpkin. Tears streamed down his face. He patted whomever he could, the love of humanity in his deformed hands. And five times he rushed in to help them, only to be grabbed by the men and taken out again. And he counted these times so proudly for the memory of his father, one to five.

While outside you could see a flame, a billow of smoke, and horses running madly about the snowy pasture and stopping up, only to bolt again straight in the dark, or coming out at you, their eyes flashing, inside it was fire and ruthless pandemonium.

And like pandemonium there was always a generous amount of quiet.

Louis, walking about in Garth's old wrestling stetson, stopped now to wonder what he had done and if he could do any more.

He kicked at a bale of hay that was not burning and looked displeased, and then saw Pumpkin's money lying nearby. He picked it up and put it in his pocket – and the feel of it relieved him for a second. He decided to go and find her and give her her money.

And he went to see if she was still inside. "Just stop shooting at us!" he said.

But he couldn't find her. He kept yelling, "Just stop shooting at us," for a long time. He searched until the smoke and terrible crawling flame drove him out.

He did not know at the moment that he would never find her again.

He decided to help with the horses. But most of the horses were out or dead by this time. Then he decided that he would start getting some water to put the fire out.

By now this seemed to be the best idea.

He joined the other men, hollering just like they were, and saying what a terrible thing a fire was.

Late that night he made his way across to the reserve. He had never been to Peter Bathurst's grand house before – that house on the hill – and now he went toward it. The wind had turned bitter and the sky had cleared. It was Good Friday. Louis was perfumed with soot, his dark eyes glassy.

He was filled with a kind of trepidation, a kind of hope, a longing to be with his grandmother, a longing to sit with Peter Bathurst and be just like him, and talk about power, and what plans they had for the future.

He didn't quite know what kind of power they would talk about. Something about the reserve and what they had done to show people who they were. He thought of Peter's braids, his dark glasses, and his camouflage pants. He thought of Peter in court after they had found him with a gill net fishing certain pools and how Tracy McCaustere had smiled knowingly and sadly at the accusations.

He thought of Peter flying to Ottawa to meet with top dogs, and how Mickey Dunn and he were going to build a large casino. Louis, of course, would do all of those things too.

Yet like most idealists he had no idea of what actually had gone on.

He came into the house through the side door, and walked along the same hallway old Bruce Walk on a Cloud had walked eighteen hours earlier with his chunks of maple. Louis did not know this, of course. He did not know he was entering a house filled with panic.

Peter Bathurst had been on the cellular phone. There were many people he could not contact, but he had managed to make some kind of sense to things.

He knew by now that Mickey Dunn was talking about him all over town. Peter, of course, would have to tell them where Louis Gatineau was, and relate how Louis set the fire, if he wanted any kind of deal. Still he would be charged with misappropriation of funds.

But if he gave himself up Tracy would be able to work something out, not only with the police but with the band. He would be charged with fraud, but not with arson, if he came clean. Suddenly he longed only for one thing – sleep.

Tracy told him that at six o'clock on Holy Thursday the investigation had started and tomorrow he would be taken into custody.

For an hour he sat motionless in the dark.

When he looked up at two-thirty in the morning, he saw Louis standing near him, looking frightened, holding a pizza in his hand. He had bought it with Pumpkin's travel money, and was wearing Garth's stetson hat.

∾

Anna drove back in the night. The air was sweetened by the smell of wild berries and the tick and chirp of crickets. She had to detour through the reserve, and saw how lonely and small it looked, with small paths leading here and there behind small tar-covered houses. It was all a horror show, a terrible thing to do to people.

Up on the hill a mile from St. Brenden's, Anna saw where they were beginning to remove earth for the new tourists' fishing and hunting chalets that they had worked out in conjunction with the federal government in lieu of a casino no one wanted. It would bring hundreds of thousands of dollars to their economy, or so they hoped.

Ms Bartibog was considered a great woman, who had achieved all of this by consensus, and she had wisely left her husband. Mr. Dunn was not involved once Diane's husband fell. He had lost everything. And his bar and tavern had mysteriously burned down last week.

Peter Bathurst was now in jail. And Mary Francis visited him twice a month. There was a certain gratitude in his eyes whenever she came – for she was the only one. And there was always hope for them, that their future together might be more meaningful than their past.

His fine house was up for sale.

Louis, one day before his trial, took Peter's 30.30 long-barrel. Went into the woods. Shot himself.

No one knew who had fired the shot at Diane Bartibog.

Far away, the remnants of the Shackle barn had been bulldozed under. The house stood empty, a "For Sale" sign in the front yard. Anna turned and drove across the bridge.

She stopped for a moment and went in. Everything was silent. Tom's hat was hanging on the hat rack behind the stove. Everything important had been removed.

Vicki had received condolences from all over North America, and some of the cards were still in a box on the counter. One was a sympathy card from Igor Rasperov, who now lived in New Jersey and had finished his hockey career there. He called Garth one of the greatest players he had ever played against.

There were cards from players all over the NHL and from Europe – for hockey was hockey – and once, just once, he had dazzled the world.

There were cards of course for Pumpkin also; a lot from the reserve, a huge one, a truthful one, from Ms Diane Bartibog. But there was nothing anyone, no matter how much they wanted to, could ever do. Vicki had placed these cards for Pumpkin inside the Louisa May Alcott book. The book had been re-covered with plastic to make it last.

The air was silent. There was a chirp of a bird, and a car passed by.

Jenna Wheem helped Vicki get back on her feet and convalesce. But Vicki had gone.

No one knew where she had gone, or where she was now or what in fact she would ever do with the life she had left to live. And no one ever saw her again. The money she had needed to get her off the hook that day had been sent by Verriker's wife and was in the bank all Holy Thursday afternoon.

No one, not even Verriker, knew this at the time.

In the summer, feeling his influence gone, both at university and in Toronto, feeling bitter with Neil's appointment on the very day he was in the woods, feeling people were too unkind to his work at Le Chateau, Wheem retired. His young fiancée left him. He took a package of so many thousands, and managed to pay his debt to the bank. He moved to Nova Scotia, where he still spoke about his writing and editing skills and his influence over writers like Dexter. He appeared on cable television as often as possible, saying he was planning a follow-up book about the Shackle tragedy. He was still always enthusiastic, in a tourist-brochure way, but something about him was missing.

There were lines in his face and around his goatee. His mouth took on a hurt appearance, as if he had been swallowed by himself and didn't know any longer what exactly to do.

Anna went home. She and Neil lived quietly. He stayed at the university late and came home to a largely darkened house. Anna began to do charity work and was considered, because of her rather Catholic views and her lame leg, somewhat of a Maritime eccentric. And as long as people dismissed her logic as eccentricity she was tolerated.

Some time passed like this. They decided not to adopt.

Late in September of that year, they received a letter from Reggie. Anna read it often. It seemed to help her for some reason.

*Down streets I have walked. I have slept with whores in places and thinking I would like to be like you – how I would like to be like my brother Neil, who was now a president at a university. Never, Neil, be like me. In all my life I have never been what I could if maybe I tried.*

*Somehow I don't think Pumpy ever had much of a life, keeping care of her grandfather, and her little pup, Folly, and waiting for someone to tell her that she too belonged. Anyway, I know that you did what you could.*

*Anyways, I come under fire five times, a mortar attack once and strafed too – the side of the APC, which is being refitted with ceramic – so listen to this. The attack came because the Serbs felt the Croats had too many sandbags about one of their guns. The Croats said the Serbs had as many sandbags as they. I had to go and check on the sandbags; me and a small private, eighteen years old, Denny Vinot, had to leave the zone and inspect both positions.*

*Counting sandbags – and of course how many sandbags did they hide. (Ha ha)*

*So here it isn't so bad. You have to watch the claymores or they will tear you in two, and no one here will care. I'm here only for the children – for the little ones – last winter we gave our rations to some – bottled water and cold meat.*

*I adopted a Muslim I called Pumpkin. I wanted to take her home with me. She was a little girl of eight with one leg. I saw a terrible thing which is what happened to Pumpkin.*

*The Serbs kept us away, for two months I didn't get to see her or bring her supplies.*

*One night I wanted to kill everyone for what has happened to Pumpkin and her little brother, but I only manage to cry. I went into the house after everyone had been driven on the road and crawling on my knees I asked forgiveness for the world. I doubt if Pumpkin heard any more.*

*I guess I still ask her forgiveness just about every day. I ask for our Pumpkin's too.*

*I am here only for Pumpkin, but I am growing old. The children are angels – everyone else is a bastard. I wish I had done something betterer or more useful with my stupid ignorant life – a sawed-off sergeant in a hopeless army!*

*May God bless, have mercy on us all.*